"I think," Ethan said, "I've come to the right place."

"Why would you think that?" A siren sounded outside.

"Here they are, too late as usual." Mel reached past him and flipped one of the three dead bolts. "I'd better go out and talk to the cops."

Ethan covered her hand with his. "Don't."

"Excuse me?"

Teeth clenched to hold back a groan, he staggered to his feet. "Leave the cops out of this."

"No way. Those men were attacking you, and you forced your way into my office. Right now, it's looking like all three of you are dangerous—and mixed up in something I want no part of. Why else would you not want me to go out to the cops?"

"I'm fine with you talking to the cops." Ethan pulled himself to his full six feet two inches and looked into the lady's eyes at least a foot lower than his. "But just don't tell them about me. If they get involved, those men you saw outside, or others like them, will hurt my sister."

Laurie Alice Eakes dreamed of being a writer from the time she was a small child. Now, with her dreams fulfilled, she is the award-winning and bestselling author of over two dozen historical and contemporary novels. When she isn't writing full-time, she enjoys long walks, live theater and being near her beloved Lake Michigan. She lives in Illinois with her husband and sundry cats and dogs.

Books by Laurie Alice Eakes

Love Inspired Suspense

Perilous Christmas Reunion
Lethal Ransom
Exposing a Killer
Abduction Rescue

Visit the Author Profile page at LoveInspired.com.

ABDUCTION RESCUE

LAURIE ALICE EAKES

LOVE INSPIRED SUSPENSE
INSPIRATIONAL ROMANCE

LOVE INSPIRED® SUSPENSE
INSPIRATIONAL ROMANCE

ISBN-13: 978-1-335-58731-2

Recycling programs
for this product may
not exist in your area.

Abduction Rescue

For questions and comments about the quality of this book, please contact us
at CustomerService@Harlequin.com.

Love Inspired
22 Adelaide St. West, 41st Floor
Toronto, Ontario M5H 4E3, Canada
www.LoveInspired.com

Printed in U.S.A.

Two are better than one;
because they have a good reward for their labour.
For if they fall, the one will lift up his fellow:
but woe to him that is alone when he falleth;
for he hath not another to help him up.
—*Ecclesiastes* 4:9-10

To Dina and Tina.

Your support and understanding means more to me than I can ever express.

ONE

Pounding on the office door yanked Melissa—Mel—Carter upright in her desk chair. Someone banging on the front office door of the private investigation agency wasn't uncommon after hours. Hammering on the door to the alley had happened only once in the four years Mel had worked at the firm.

Once too often. Once had been enough to teach Mel not to open that door, no matter how urgent the knocking sounded. Someone with a gun could be lurking on the other side. That time, it had been a disgruntled man whose life had been turned upside down by the information the PIs had uncovered. A man with a gun he hadn't been afraid to use.

Mel clamped her hand to her side. Her wounds had healed. The physical ones, at least. The scars on her spirit might never go away.

"I'll just ignore it," she said aloud, the sound of her voice eerie in the empty office. "Ignore… Ignore…"

She was good at ignoring nowadays—ignoring fear, ignoring worry, ignoring the way she always felt as though she had forgotten something because she no longer carried her gun. She'd been wearing it when she'd opened the door to the husband caught cheating on his wife. He had aimed his gun at her and pulled the trigger.

And when she'd realized her life was in danger, she'd drawn and fired as well.

His bullet had plowed through her side, nicked a rib, missed a kidney by a millimeter. Mel's bullet had struck him in the chest.

He was still alive—with one lung and a long prison term before him. Mel was still alive and unwilling to ever come so close again to killing another human being. No more guns for her. Not ever again.

She ignored the repeated hammering on the alleyway door and stared at the computer screen in front of her. Megan, her boss, needed information by morning; one of the reasons Mel was working late. The other reason, the one she wouldn't admit to, was that she didn't like going home to her empty house. When she could bury herself in her work, it was easier to ignore her loneliness. But it was impossible to concentrate when the insistent bang, bang, bang on the back door struck right through Mel's head.

And suddenly it stopped. One moment, she'd thought she'd heard a shout along with the volley of knocks, and the next instant, nothing. The alley had become as quiet as the office was dark beyond Mel's cubicle.

That brought her to her feet, reaching for her purse. She might not carry her gun, but she carried pepper spray and a key chain alarm loud enough to drown a tornado siren.

The silence outside was as portentous as the weather before a bad storm.

Maintaining her silence, Mel tiptoed to the door in her sneakers. Not a single window looked onto the alley. Not even a peephole in the door.

With no way to look without opening the door, Mel laid her ear against the steel panel. She heard the low rumble of traffic on Belmont a half block away, the clatter of a dumpster lid…

And then a single, solid thud against the door. A cry of pain followed.

"Where is it?" someone shouted from a distance.

The answer, which seemed to be coming from right on the other side of the alley door, was too soft for Mel to hear. Something negative, no doubt, since the first guy yelled back, "Not good enough. Where is it?"

Mel flattened herself against the door, heart racing. Mind racing. The shouts and soft responses outside continued. Her head flashed with a memory of other shouts outside the door. *Where is she? Where is she?*

That man had had a gun. No shots here. Not now. One man sounded angry enough to have used his if he'd had one. The other either didn't have the strength to speak loudly or refused to do so.

Speak softly to diffuse anger.

It hadn't worked that night. Mel had whispered to the angry cheating spouse, and he had still shot her.

"This is not the same," she told herself. "This is an argument. Not your fight."

Yet someone had been pounding on the door—a frantic pounding. They'd wanted in. For safety?

"Do you want your left knee to look like your right?" one man demanded.

Not just an argument—a fight. Physical harm, even

if it didn't include guns. That cry of pain. That thud against the door as though someone had fallen into it.

Someone was being assaulted outside her door, and she was cowering like a coward.

Mel dragged her purse from beneath her to inspect its contents. Wallet. Pepper spray. Phone.

She pressed the side button on her cell. "Call 9—"

A crash sounded beyond the door. A rumbling, hollow clang of metal striking metal. She knew that noise—it was not uncommon in a narrow alleyway lined with wheeled dumpsters.

Something heavy had plowed into the one right outside the office. Right next to where the person had fallen against the door.

Guns or not, this man's life was in danger.

"Call 9-1-1," she got out this time.

"Chicago 9-1-1. What is your emergency?" a nearly mechanical voice inquired.

Not her emergency, someone else's.

"Fight in the alley behind…" She gave the address while listening for the violence to escalate.

"Stay on the line and remain at a distance," the dispatcher advised.

Good advice. This wasn't her fight. But her stint at the police academy had taught her to respond to people in crisis. Even if she had gone on to become a private investigator rather than don a blue uniform, she couldn't turn away from people in trouble.

She rose to her knees and flipped the three dead bolts on the door. Pepper spray in one hand and key chain with the alarm in the other, she stood and twisted the knob.

Headlights flared into her eyes the instant the door

opened—headlights from a sports car a mere yard away. The engine revved. The dumpster had been crammed against the bricks to one side, and a man holding a blackjack blocked the exit from the other side. These men had positioned themselves to trap someone in place.

And their target was the man slumped against her feet.

For an instant when the support of the door disappeared from his back, Ethan McClure was nearly flat on his rear. He tucked his knees to his chest and rolled sideways, landing on his feet behind the now-open steel door. His right knee buckled, the artificial joint not quite up to such acrobatics even after five years since a roadside bomb had forced him to leave the original joint in Afghanistan. He grasped the door with one hand for balance, then tried to pull the lady back from the threshold with the other.

If they got inside, slammed the door, lock—

"Let go of me." The lady was small, but as supple and agile as a cat. She twisted around out of his grasp, stepping farther from the office and closer to danger.

Ethan's stomach sank as Steel Toes lunged toward the doorway. The driver of the sports car stepped on the gas.

And the woman spray-blasted Steel Toes with a face full of capsaicin.

The man screeched like a scalded cat and rolled over the low hood of the car, jumping into the back seat. A door slammed. The engine revved, and the car sped down the alley.

"You go too." Ms. Pepper Spray faced Ethan, stepping back into the office and letting the door slip half-shut behind her. The can she held up was so small, he doubted it contained more of its weapon. But he wasn't taking a chance. He snatched it from her fingers.

And she kicked him in his knee. His weak knee, which was already shaky after his run from the men sent to extract information from him. This time, he couldn't maintain his balance when the knee buckled. He landed on it hard, an involuntary oof escaping.

The lady stared at him, eyes wide. Her lips moved, but Ethan couldn't hear what she said over the roar of the sports car's engine as the driver tried turning the vehicle in the narrow alleyway.

Ethan shoved the door all the way shut and reached for the lock.

"What are you doing?" the lady demanded.

"Locking out the bad guys." Once the door was secure, with all three bolts in place, Ethan resisted the urge to slump against it and cradle his knee in both hands. He couldn't let his guard down quite yet—not when this woman had already proved she could lay him low.

She may not look like much of a threat, given that she wasn't any bigger than a minute, with huge deep brown eyes framed by short white-blond hair. But the way she held herself—still, watchful, wary—and the way she hadn't hesitated to strike when the situation demanded action, made it clear that she had training and she wasn't afraid to use it.

"I think," he said, "I have come to the right place."

"Why would you think that?" She reached for a key chain hanging from her purse strap. He recognized the extra little fob just as a siren sounded outside, rising above even the diminishing roar of the sports car's engine.

"Here they are, too late as usual." She reached past him and flipped one of the three dead bolts. "I'd better go out and talk to the cops so they don't think I prank called them. You need to file a report too."

Ethan covered her hand with his. "Don't."

"Excuse me?" She lifted that little fob with her other hand.

"Don't press that alarm either." Teeth clenched to hold back a groan, he staggered to his feet. "Leave the cops out of this."

"No way."

"Please." He smiled now, trying to imbue it with any charm he might possess.

"Uh-uh." She shook her head. "Those men were attacking you, and you forced your way into my office. Right now, it's looking like all three of you are dangerous—and mixed up in something I want no part of. Why else would you not want me to go out to the cops?"

"I'm fine with you talking to the cops." Ethan pulled himself to his full six-foot-two-inch height and looked into the lady's eyes at least a foot lower than his. "But just don't tell them about me. If they get involved, those men you saw outside or others like them will hurt my sister."

TWO

Mel gazed at the man who stood before her. Although he'd just made a shocking announcement, he appeared as composed as a marble statue. *Stoic*, she thought. And polite, if she ignored how he had entered her office against her will.

She should probably turn this whole mess over to the police. If his sister was in danger, they could keep her safe. And yet—

"Thanks for rescuing me." He interrupted her contemplations.

His voice was gentle, deep, with an accent suggesting he came from somewhere farther south than the Ohio River.

"It's a bad habit of mine." Mel grimaced. "Everything from kittens to men being bullied in the alley." She frowned at his face. A nice face. Better than nice. Strong cheekbones and a square jaw. Laugh lines by his wide mouth and at the corners of his eyes, all highlighted by thick, chestnut hair.

And a bruise forming on the side of his jaw.

"Did they hit you?" she asked.

"Just a tap." He fingered the swelling.

Mel remembered the thud against the door and made a decision.

"Come sit in my cubicle, and I'll get you an ice-pack for that bruise while you tell me what you mean about someone hurting your sister."

"You seem pretty calm about all that."

"In my work, I have to be calm about everything, or bad things can happen."

"They still do sometimes, don't they?" It was phrased as a question, but it was clear he already knew the answer.

About to turn toward the hallway, she paused and looked at him. "You know who I am?"

"I read the *Tribune* even in my little town." He smiled.

Argh. It was a nice smile. A kind smile to go along with the gentleness in his gray-green eyes.

Stay on your guard, she reminded herself.

"I can guess what you read." She grimaced and led the way to her cubicle. "They made me out to be some kind of superwoman heroine."

"You're not?" He sounded dismayed.

She glanced back and noticed a twinkle in his eyes. She also noticed he was limping badly.

Of course, he was. She had given him a good kick on his knee.

"Have a seat." She indicated the chair across from her desk.

He dropped into it immediately.

"How about some ice for your knee too?"

He inclined his head. "That would be kind of you."

"It's the least I can do after kicking you."

All the same, she wasn't going to apologize for defending herself. After all, in the moment when she'd struck, he'd just locked himself inside with her and had wrenched the pepper spray out of her hand. Kicking was an appropriate response. But he hadn't made a single aggressive move toward her since then, which had her inclined to believe he didn't intend to hurt her. He might even be telling the truth about being an ordinary guy trying to protect his sister. She would hear him out, if nothing else.

From the kitchen, she grabbed two bottles of water from the refrigerator and two icepacks from the freezer. First aid in hand, she returned to her cubicle. The water she placed on either side of the desk. The icepacks she set in the man's hands.

"I'm Mel, by the way," she said, though he must already know.

"Melissa Carter," he said.

She wrinkled her nose. "I prefer Mel. Melissa sounds like I should be baking cupcakes, not tracking down bad guys."

Except she no longer tracked down bad guys. Not directly, anyway. These days, she was the researcher who left the more dangerous side of the business to her boss.

That charming smile again, lighting the dimly lit office. "Ethan McClure. I go by Ethan."

It suited him. Strong. Masculine.

"And I do bake cupcakes," he added.

Mel lowered herself into her chair, trying not to stare. She knew they existed, but had never met a man who baked cupcakes or even so much as a frozen pizza for himself. A pity he seemed to carry trouble with him. She could like him.

"That's admirable. But you didn't come here to discuss cupcakes." She retreated behind her business-like façade.

"No, ma'am. I—"

"Wait." Mel held up a hand. "Please stop calling me ma'am. I'm only twenty-seven. At least wait until I'm thirty before you start that ma'aming stuff. I'm just Mel."

"Yes, ma—um, sure." He laid one icepack across his knee and held the other to his jaw. "I'll try to re-member." His eyes lost their twinkle, shining more gray than green. "I came here for help, for my sister. You see, she was kidnapped two days ago."

"If she was kidnapped, you should contact the police." Her response was immediate.

He wasn't the first family member to come to the agency asking for no law enforcement help with a kidnapping.

"As a PI firm, we can't get involved with a kidnapping," she explained. "It's too risky."

"So is getting law enforcement involved."

Mel tried not to sigh. A little puff of exasperation slipped out.

She twisted off the cap of her bottle and swallowed a long draft of the cold water before speaking slowly. "The local police have more resources to handle this kind of situation."

"It wouldn't be their jurisdiction, even if I was willing to bring them in," Ethan said. "The crime crossed state lines."

Of course. The accent.

"Kentucky," he added. "McClure."

Her eyebrows shot up, surprised to hear that the

town was named for his family. She'd have expected someone with that kind of background to be…fancier, somehow. Instead, he wore ordinary clothes that could have been bought at any retail store in any mall in the country. Plain, light blue, button-down shirt and jeans. Hiking boots. Comfortable. Fitting well.

She yanked her mind from the way his shirt stretched across his broad shoulders and focused on the issue at hand.

"I still don't see how we can help you." She held up one hand, palm toward him. "Let me tell you, first off, that we will not help with a ransom drop."

"There's no ransom."

"I beg your pardon?"

"Those men out there?" He gestured toward the alley. "They want information. Very valuable information."

"And what information is that?"

"Where about half a million dollars in drug money is hidden."

She tried not to gulp. Definitely a case for the cops, not the agency. The stakes were too high. Too risky. Too…unbelievable.

"I think you should stop there," she began. "The police—"

"No." Sharp as a hammer blow. "I don't trust—"

Pounding on the back door interrupted his declaration. Through the steel panel, the muffled voice sounded like a shout.

"Police!"

Ethan locked his gaze with Mel Carter's, silently pleading with her not to answer that imperious call.

She stood. "I called them. I need to answer."

For a moment of rashness, Ethan considered clutching her hand for one more chance to beg her not to share what he had just told her. But he had no right to touch her, let alone restrain her.

"Please," was all he managed to say before she whisked out of the cubicle and along the hallway.

Hands pressed to the top of the desk, he sat, waiting. Twenty feet away, the dead bolts clicked.

"Yes, Officer." Mel's voice carried over the tops of the cubicle dividers. "Are you here about the 9-1-1 call?" She sounded calm, emotionless.

"Yes, ma'am. Did you call?" The officer sounded older, even kind.

Ethan did not relax.

"I called. There was a fight in the alley. Sounded like a group ganging up on someone." Mel's inhale was loud enough to carry to her cubicle, to Ethan's ears. "But they seem to have cleared out."

"Do you know if any weapons were involved?" the officer asked.

"I didn't hear any shots fired." Her voice changed, tightened.

"Did you see anything?" Another voice spoke up, a young, female voice.

"As you can see, there's no window," Mel said. It was the truth, even if it was misleading. "I heard some yelling and a few thuds. But they took off when they heard a siren. I heard their car drive away."

A moment of silence followed.

"What about the man who was being assaulted?" the female cop asked.

Another pause. Too long. The moment when she would admit he sat in her office.

"He was able to walk away." Mel spoke too slowly.

Again, she had stretched the truth…for him.

Why?

"I see." The older cop seemed dubious. "Give us another call if you hear anything else."

"Thanks for checking up." Mel closed the door with a decisive bang. Locks clicked. Then nothing. No footfalls sounded on the floor. No other sounds filled the stillness of the office for several minutes.

Ethan held his breath, half expecting her to open the door and call the officers back.

Then she appeared in the opening of the cubicle. "They're gone." She sounded—angry. No, annoyed was more accurate.

"What you tell me next had better be convincing," she said, "because that's the first time I've been less than honest with a cop in my life."

"Thank you for that." Ethan inclined his head. "I'll do my best to explain, but…it's hard to know where to begin."

Unable to look directly at her, he shifted his gaze to the partition behind her. Pictures of a man and woman in police uniforms hung on the felt wall, surrounded by photographs of six cats, each in its own silver frame.

He wanted to ask her about the pictures. He wanted to ask her about the shooting in March—not least because the write-up of that incident had made him believe he could trust her, that she was the one who could help him get this job done. He wanted to ask her anything but whether or not she would help him.

He didn't want her to have the opportunity to say no.

"Let me ask you a few questions then," she suggested.

Ethan returned his gaze to her face, relaxed now. "Shoot," he said.

"That would be difficult." Her tone was dry, her lips turned up at the corners. "I don't carry a gun," she said. Her hint of a smile fell. "Anymore."

He nodded, guessing why she no longer carried a gun. Shooting a man, even nonfatally, was traumatic for anyone.

"Me either." He set the now-warm icepack on the desk, so he had both hands free. "I've seen more than enough death."

Her eyes widened.

"I was military police for ten years," he explained.

"You didn't want to go for career status?" she asked.

"Invalided out." He tapped his right knee. "So much shrapnel in my knee, they had to replace the joint. Wasn't my plan, but it worked out in the end. I got home in time to help my family."

"Wife and kids?" For some reason, she colored at her query.

The delicate pink enhanced the deep brown of her eyes. Sable brown. Such an unusual and lovely contrast with her pale blond hair.

"No wife or kids. My parents and younger sister and her boys." Thoughts of the children warmed him, and he smiled. "Twin boys. They're five. And they need their mother to come home safely."

She sighed. "Please don't try to manipulate me."

Despite his aching knee, despite anxiety over his

sister's whereabouts and the danger she was in, Ethan had to suppress a chuckle at her irritation.

"Not manipulation," he said. "Just truth."

"Then go on with the rest of the truth. What happened? Start at the beginning." She leaned back in her chair, folding her arms across her middle.

Ethan leaned forward, forearms on the desk, fingers steepled. "Six years ago, my sister decided she wanted life in the big city. She couldn't be satisfied with Louisville. She came to Chicago to look for a job. Instead, she found love."

"That wasn't smart," Mel muttered.

"Definitely not with the one she found. I asked her to bring him home to meet us, but she got married first." He scrubbed his hands on his face. "She seemed happy for a while, especially once she found out she was having twins. But then she called one night, all crying and carrying on so hard, we could hardly understand her."

"He wasn't all he'd cracked up to be," Mel concluded.

Ethan nodded. "She discovered his 'good job,' which let them have such a comfortable life, was dealing drugs."

"Poor kid." Mel compressed her lips.

"Yup. Poor naïve kid. I offered to come get her, but she said she needed to do something first."

"Which was?"

"Get him arrested. She provoked him into it—let him catch her packing up the baby things she'd bought, knowing that her leaving him would set him off. He hit her." His stomach churned at the memory of learning that detail. "She called the cops on him."

"And your brother-in-law?"

"Ended up in jail. Sheila had managed to find where he was hiding some of his stash, and when the police arrived, she directed them to it. Derek was arrested—for assault and possession. He only got a few years with the possibility of parole." Ethan swallowed. "After that, she came home. What we didn't realize—what she didn't tell us at the time—was that she'd hidden something first. Specifically, her husband's stash of money he was waiting to get laundered or pay his supplier with or something."

Mel stared at him, blinking long, darkened lashes. "And now he's out on parole, and he's got her, to force her to say where she hid the money."

"I see why you're an investigator. You figured that out right quick."

"But what happened to her? And if she never told you about the money she took, then how did you find out about it?"

"Two days ago, I got a phone call from Sheila. She was in a panic because she'd just spotted him on the street. She didn't know he'd been released from prison. No one up here had told her down in Kentucky. They were supposed to, but they didn't. If she'd known he was free, she never would have gone out on her own.

"She was out buying groceries, and there he was. She had just long enough to call me, tell me that she'd seen him, that he was coming after her—and then she started spouting off a string of numbers. She didn't even get a chance to tell me what they meant before he got to her and grabbed the phone. That's how I found out about the money. He told me what she'd done—that she'd taken it and hidden it somewhere in Chicago—and that she wouldn't be released until he got his money back."

"Do you think he'll release her if she turns it over?"

"No, I think he'll kill her. But if she *doesn't* turn it over… I don't want to think of what he might do. He's already showed he has no qualms about hitting her. It wouldn't surprise me at all if he decides to torture the answers out of her. That's why I *need* to find her—and as soon as possible."

"Do you know where she is?"

"Not a clue, except for those numbers. But they could mean anything. An address, a license plate, part of a phone number." Suddenly weary beyond words, Ethan rested his head on one fist. "I have to find her. Those boys have a no-account for their father. They need their mother. My daddy's not well, and all this worry is bad for his heart." He closed his eyes to conceal the depth of his fear for his father, for his sister, for how even one death would damage them all. "I gotta save her, Miss Mel. If there's any way…"

The silence and stillness inside the agency emphasized the roar of traffic and people half a block away. Ethan figured Mel's quiet meant she was thinking.

Or maybe Mel was trying to find a nice way to say once again she couldn't possibly help him.

When he heard her take a deep inhalation, he braced himself for the worst.

"We don't take on cases here until Megan, the owner, approves them. Some cases she thinks are too dangerous or just not worth our time."

Then call her and ask her, Ethan wanted to shout.

He waited.

"That usually takes about three days, since she has to find time to review the facts in between working on her current cases," Mel continued. "Given that you're in a hurry, and have so little information, I'm just not sure we're the best option for you."

"Two, five, seven, six, three," Ethan said, as though mentioning the numbers would unlock some secret information vault.

"Not an address." Mel shook her head. "Not in the city anyway. Nothing in the city has a five-digit number—except for zip codes, of course, but that's not a US code. It could be a license plate, part of a phone number, maybe even a safe-deposit box number, if Sheila was trying to tell you where she'd hidden the money." She sipped water, sipped again. Stalling tactic. "Can you think of anything else? Even if it doesn't make sense?"

"No. Well, maybe." Ethan massaged his right leg. He rubbed his temples. His leg still throbbed. His head ached.

He pressed his fingertips to his eyes, dry and sore with fatigue. "I can only hear her screaming."

"What about her vehicle? Did Derek use it to get away?"

Ethan shook his head. "Sheila was in my truck. It was left at the store parking lot."

"And no one saw anything?"

"A gas station clerk across the street said he saw a blue sedan of some kind at the station the same time Sheila came in to get the milk. He thought the driver was going to get gas and run, so was watching the car."

"That's something to go on." She flipped up the

top of her laptop and began to tap on the keys with the speed of a machine gun.

With an effort, he held his questions until she glanced up. "Did you find anything?"

"I found that the number Sheila gave you can't be matched to any license plate in Illinois. I don't know if other states have more numbers than letters, like we do here. So maybe it's an address in the suburbs. We have hundreds of suburbs, so if you can't think of anything else…"

She trailed off, but he knew what she was trying to convey. Without more information, she couldn't help him. "I still believe your best option is to go to the cops," Mel concluded.

"How long have you lived here, Miss Mel?" He made her hold his gaze.

"I've never lived anywhere else."

"And you have family in law enforcement."

"I…did." She bit her lip and looked away.

"I mean no disrespect to your family," Ethan said carefully. "But my experience with Chicago cops comes from what Sheila's told me…and most of it isn't good. From what she said, it sounded like Derek had at least a few officers in his pocket. That's why I don't want the police looking into Sheila's case—not even the FBI. I don't know for sure that he's paid off federal agents, but it wouldn't surprise me. Either way, if word gets out to law enforcement, it would be too easy for it to get back to Derek that the authorities are poking around, trying to find Sheila and looking for the money. And if he got angry at the news, he'd take it out on my sister."

Mel winced. "I know what you're saying. Most cops are honest. It only takes one who isn't."

"That's why it took so long for Sheila to get free of him. At first, she'd tried to call in anonymous tips, hoping a drug raid would see him locked up. But his informants always warned him in advance. That's why she provoked him into hitting her. The cops who showed up weren't part of Derek's informants, so he got busted."

"Your sister may have bad taste in husbands, but she seems pretty smart when it comes to strategy, even if it's a bit dangerous."

"She's the smartest one of the family." He couldn't hold back the pride he felt for his sister and all she'd accomplished in spite of her poor romantic decisions.

Mel puffed a long breath from between pursed lips.

Ethan held her gaze again, waiting for her response, whether she would help him or leave him on his own to find and save his sister.

If more men like those in the alley didn't find him and use him as bait first.

THREE

After a night of thinking, pacing, and researching on her computer, Mel called Megan as early as she dared the next morning. Megan was younger than Mel, but seemed to have investigation in her DNA. She was smart and kind, and the best boss ever.

She was not happy with Mel's story.

"We can't get involved with a kidnapping," Megan declared. "That's a job for the feds."

"But he has good reason not to trust the authorities," Mel protested. "And besides, he's working against the clock. The longer it takes to find his sister, the more damage she'll take from her ex. And we both know that the feds aren't exactly fast when it comes to mobilizing."

"Then he should have—" Megan started to say but cut herself off by yawning. "Sorry. Up late at a cake tasting."

"Seriously? The lady who never wears anything but jeans and T-shirts is having a wedding fancy enough to require a cake tasting?"

Megan sighed. "I never should have promised my mother she could have full rein over my wedding. It's going to be ridiculously over the top."

"I knew that the minute you asked me to put on that Cinderella ball gown you called a bridesmaid's dress. I'm going to look like a joke."

"You're going to look beautiful." Megan yawned again. "Anyway, I couldn't sleep after all that sugar, then had a dress fitting at seven o'clock this morning, so I'm running on basically no sleep."

"I'm so glad I've decided to never marry."

Megan snorted. "Once bitten twice shy?"

A chill ran through Mel at painful memories. "I was more than bitten. I mean I wasn't actually bitten…" She had thought she'd found the love of her life once upon a time. He had broken more than her heart.

But he hadn't broken her spirit.

She cleared her throat. "Back to the point. Seriously, Megan, he's got nowhere else to go, and he's really worried. Just let me try to figure out what those numbers he got from his sister mean."

She would see what that led to and work from there on the research side of things. She didn't want to be in the middle of potential violence any more than Megan and Jack wanted her in the middle of violence. She had seen enough of that for a lifetime.

"He needs help, and I can't force him to go to any kind of authority."

Megan sighed. "Mel… If I could spare anyone… but… Okay. You can see where those numbers lead, which will be nowhere, I expect. But keep your guard up, all right? This one sounds like it could be tricky. I don't want you landing yourself in danger."

Mel thanked her friend and assured her she'd be careful. Then she turned to her computer with only a twinge of guilt for what had popped up on her screen the minute she'd woken it up.

She had three possibilities as to the location connected to Ethan McClure's sister since she hadn't actually waited for Megan's approval before starting her search.

She reached for her phone and pulled up Ethan on her contacts.

He answered before the first ring finished. "Miss Mel."

Mel ground her teeth. "Mel."

He should at least know better than to call her *Miss* Mel.

"I can help you with the numbers," she announced without preamble.

"How?"

Mel liked the way he didn't waste time or words on expressing surprise or asking if she was sure. He got right to the point.

"I found three possibilities outside the city." She took a breath and started to explain.

"Where can I meet you?" he asked in the moment of her silence.

"You want to meet me to check them out?"

"Yes, ma'am."

"I warned you not to call me ma'am."

"Beg pardon, ma'am. I mean—"

"Mel will do. We're not formal here, remember?"

"I've been raised to treat everyone with courtesy. Hard to break a thirty-six-year-old habit."

So, he was thirty-six. Not that that mattered to Mel.

"I'll pick you up," she said. "I need to do the driving."

"I suppose that makes sense, you knowing your way around and all."

"For more reasons than one."

If they were followed today, she wanted to be in the driver's seat. She knew all the back roads and major highways like they were the lines on her palms. She could get away from anyone, even in broad daylight.

"You think those men from last night are watching us," Ethan said.

"I think we have a distinct likelihood of being followed. If Derek's men think you're trying to rescue Sheila before she can be forced to turn over the money, then they'll be determined to stop you. Of course, if they think that she told you where the money is, then they might want to capture you as well—either to force you to talk or to use you as leverage against Sheila."

Considering what she'd overheard the previous night, she thought that might be what the men had been attempting in the alley. If they'd just wanted to kill Ethan, they could have done so easily. No, they'd wanted him alive. Having *two* people in their custody who knew the location of the money would give them a lot more leeway to get violent. After all, they only needed *one* person to live long enough to give them answers.

"Either way," she said briskly, pushing the thought aside, "I'll do everything I know to avoid getting cornered by them."

"That's a right fine goal, Miss Mel." He paused long enough for Mel to hear the wail of a siren from his end of the call. "Because if they catch us, whether they decide to kill me or bring me in, they're not going to want any witnesses. Which means you—" He stopped.

She didn't need him to finish. She had already figured it out.

If Ethan's brother-in-law and his goons caught Ethan while he was with her, she would be collateral damage.

Ethan waited inside the foyer of the bed-and-breakfast where he could see Mel's car the instant she pulled to the curb. He couldn't help thinking he shouldn't have let her help him this far. He should have told her to give him the information she had found and let her go about her business away from the danger, especially when they both knew how serious—how deadly—the danger was. It was one thing for him to face it. This was his family, after all, and it was his responsibility to keep them safe and protected. But this wasn't Mel's fight.

Too late now. She was pulling up to the curb, her small car an unassuming gray in the clear light.

He opened the door and sprinted to the car.

She leaned across to open the passenger door, and he slid in, nearly bumping his head on the top of the doorframe.

"Careful. It's low." She pulled away from the curb before he had his door shut. "Now get your seat belt on and hang on. I think I was followed here."

The instant his belt snapped into place, she touched her foot to the gas pedal and spun around a corner that would have had any taller vehicle tipping to the side. Ethan held on—literally. One hand gripped the armrest, the other the console. His eyes stayed fixed on the rearview mirror.

He saw…nothing. Nothing in the way of cars in pursuit, that was. He spotted a blur of buildings, the disapproving glances of a couple of older women, and the admiring looks of a handful of young men.

Mel twisted the wheel and they squealed beneath the tracks of an L line.

She darted down random alleys and back onto quiet side streets for the next fifteen minutes. Then, suddenly, they were winding up the entrance ramp to a highway and entering the flow of traffic at an average speed for the right-hand lane.

"Lost them." She grinned.

"I never saw them," Ethan admitted, "though I expected the police to run you down."

She shrugged. "Nah, I know where to drive not to get caught." Her gaze flicked from the road and traffic ahead to the rearview mirror then back to the highway. "They were following us just far enough back, you had to know where to look to spot them."

"I see." Ethan released his holds on the console and armrest. "What were they driving?"

"A black Charger."

He gripped his knees and twisted so he could peer around the headrest. "You drive. I'll keep watch."

"So, you believe me?"

"I do. But how did you outrun a Charger?"

"Same engine." She patted the dashboard. "This may look like an innocent little sedan, but my dad and I modified it."

"For the Indianapolis 500?"

Her only answer was a mysterious smile.

Ethan shifted his focus to the windows and the rearview mirror. He'd never noticed so many black cars on the road before now, when one might mean pursuit and whatever Derek's own enemies had planned next.

He had to find Sheila before he was too late. Derek needed her alive to get answers from her...but Ethan wouldn't put it past him to do enough damage to leave her permanently, painfully, changed. A body could go through a horrifying amount of damage without actually dying. She didn't deserve to pay for her past mistakes in such a terrible way.

The next half hour or so passed without another word being spoken as they transitioned from the highway onto a quieter road. The silence filling the car seemed profound. The engine to her vehicle purred with perfectly tuned precision, soothing under other circumstances, frustrating in this one. It proclaimed power to go faster. Posted signs proclaimed the need to remain at a steady pace.

"Ethan." Her voice intruded on his thoughts. "Do you see…"

"Yes," he answered. "I see."

A black Charger followed way too close behind them. As in tailgating close. Apparently, the driver had decided to stop being discreet.

"If you stop quick, he'll be in the back seat," Ethan drawled.

"Then hang on to your hat."

"Do you think—" Ethan didn't bother to finish his question as the car swooped ahead as though it had just acquired wings. Ethan glanced at the speedometer then wished he hadn't. He didn't mind going eighty. He minded going eighty on a road that curved, even if the land itself was flat. And they had passed eighty.

But so had the Charger. At first, it fell back, but then it began to gain on them. Half a mile. Quarter mile. The length of a football field.

Mel sped around another curve, pedal to the metal. Ethan's stomach dropped in the other direction. The

Charger blazed behind them, just as powerful, just as fast.

"What's he trying to prove?" Mel asked.

"It's bigger than we are. Maybe the plan is to run us off the road?"

"If he messes up my car—" Mel didn't finish the implied threat and took a corner on two wheels.

Twisted in his seat to look behind, Ethan bumped against her in the narrow confines of the cab, jerking her hand on the wheel. The car swerved. Ditches lined the roads on either side. For half a moment, the right front wheel hovered over the edge of one. Mel straightened them out, but the maneuver forced her to slow down and, in that instant, they lost ground. Precious ground. The Charger gained. With the roar of its engine, the larger vehicle closed inch by inch. No more turnoffs here. They had reached the country. Open fields, a half-finished subdivision with mostly basement holes and rutted tracks where streets would be.

The Charger was now only ten yards behind them, and still gaining. Five yards. Three. Its bumper drew level with their rear one. Light glinted off the windshield, blocking a clear view into the driver's face.

The blow didn't come. Instead, the right front window lowered.

"Duck!" Ethan shouted.

He pushed Mel's head toward the steering wheel and grabbed it himself, head down as far as he could get it as the left window exploded into chunks of safety glass.

FOUR

Mel couldn't breathe. Ethan held her so her face pressed against her knee. Pressure on her knee placed weight on her foot. In turn, her foot stomped the gas pedal to the floor, to full throttle. With a Hemi engine, that meant they were going fast. Way too fast when the driver couldn't see where the car was headed.

Hands holding the steering wheel with a death grip, Mel had no idea whether she should turn it one way or the other or hold it straight. She doubted the direction mattered. At their current speed, it wouldn't take long before they would crash into *something*. Anything. Brick wall or concrete foundation. They might flip, roll, end up on fire.

She needed to regain control of her vehicle. Yet doing so, sitting upright where she could see through the windshield, risked her getting shot.

It was a risk she had to take. The shooter wouldn't be able to aim well at his current speed.

"I can't breathe," Mel said. Her lungs weren't built to be so compressed.

"Sorry." Ethan moved so she could sit up. "I think

they may be gone," he said. "At least, I can't see them at the moment. *Brake!*"

The last word he shouted as though she were twenty feet away, not mere inches.

She tried swinging her right foot to the brake. It wouldn't move fast enough. Tension and fear had her body feeling like it had been twisted into knots, and it was slow to respond to her brain's commands. Eventually, she managed to press her left foot on the brake. Though it felt like an hour, she knew mere seconds had passed since Ethan told her to brake. It still wasn't fast enough. Her tires spun on loose gravel, caught. The engine roared in protest.

And then they crashed.

The car stopped as though a giant hand had grabbed it and held it in place. Mel expected to feel her head smash into the dashboard and knock her silly. But a hand had intervened, curving around the top of her head to protect it from impact. Ethan's fingers must be throbbing, but he made no sound of pain. The only sounds were the engine grumbling like an annoyed hound, and a pattering noise on the roof and hood. Was that rain? But how could it be? Moments ago, there had been nothing but a pure blue sky.

Mel lifted her head at last. Not rain—dirt. Particles covered the windshield and poured through the broken window.

"You took out a mountain of dirt," Ethan said. "Looks like they were digging to put in the foundations for a new house." He seemed calmer than Mel felt. Her teeth chattered and her body shook as though the shower of dirt were a blast of an ice storm.

"We drove right onto a construction site. It could

have been a mountain of bricks," she murmured. "Bricks would have—"

"Never mind that." Ethan touched her arm. "It wasn't bricks. We're not crushed. Let's try to back out of here."

Mel tried. She had gotten herself out of deep snow. She had worked herself out of a ditch once. She had even gotten the car out of mud as pernicious as quicksand. But she couldn't work them out of this dirt mountain. The front end was buried too deep. Moving either forward or backward seemed to do nothing but dig them deeper.

"We can't stay here." Mel said.

"Are you all right to move?" Ethan already had his door open.

He'd been waiting for her. She was the one supposed to be helping him, yet he was the one keeping his cool.

Good thing she hadn't become a cop.

"I'm good."

As in, she was able to think and move now.

She tried to push her door open. Nothing happened. She threw her entire weight against it. The door stuck fast.

A glance through the shattered side window told her why. Dirt reached halfway up the door. She would need a shovel to dig the car out.

"I'll crawl across," she said.

She had to do that or crawl over what was left of the window. The window through which someone had shot a bullet or more.

Don't think about it.

She would fall apart again if she let herself dwell on those gunshots, the shattering glass, Ethan saving her from harm...

"Need a hand?" he asked.

She shook her head. She could manage this. The car was small. So was she. She swung her legs over the console and slid across the seat. It was light gray— now with flecks of rust. Blood. Ethan was bleeding from various nicks and scrapes after being showered with broken glass. He was not bleeding badly. Not in streams. But bleeding, nonetheless. And he hadn't made a single word of protest.

Her feet on the ground, she scanned her car from bumper to bumper. Or what she hoped was bumper somewhere beneath a mound of soil. As far as she could tell with only half of it visible, it was totaled.

Her eyes pricked with tears. She shook her head to deny the pain of loss. This was only a car. No one should put so much love into a thing like a car. People were more important. People like Ethan and his sister, who needed her help.

Yet the car was the last thing she and her father had worked on together. They'd taken it for a cruise along Lake Shore Drive, Lake Michigan smelling clean and cold in the autumnal air…

And the next day, an escaped inmate had shot her father through the heart while he'd tried to restrain the man.

She bowed her head so Ethan couldn't see her tears. "Maybe we can salvage the engine later."

"We'll have to salvage ourselves now. The driver could come after us." For some reason, Ethan's drawl seemed more intense. Maybe his accent got stronger when his adrenaline was high.

"Yeah." She nodded too hard. "We need to get ourselves out of here."

Head still bowed, Mel headed away from her car, toward the edge of the dirt mountain to where they could see the road. The construction site was quiet. No equipment ran at that moment. No workers to help them, but also no motors roared to signal that their attacker's car was approaching. The bad guys could have come after her and Ethan, attacked them again while they were sitting ducks stuck in the soil. But they hadn't.

That made her more uneasy than if she heard the ratchet of a cocking gun.

Glancing up, she caught a glimpse of the road not far off.

"Do you think they're waiting to ambush us?" She figured Ethan would know about reconnaissance. He was former military. Or so he'd said.

He stopped, holding up an arm like a railroad barricade. "Their car's still on the road."

He had the advantage of at least a foot of height on her. Even on tiptoe, sinking into the dirt, Mel could barely see over a nearby pile of cinder blocks.

A good thing they hadn't run into those. The Lord was looking out for them.

She hugged her arms across her middle, holding in the pain. "What are they doing?"

"I don't know." Ethan held his hand as a shield for his eyes. "I don't see any movement near the Charger."

Mel rubbed her arms. No movement probably meant they were out of the car, hunting. Mel didn't like being prey, but at the moment, she didn't have much choice. She had no idea what they might be up against—how many people, how well armed, how well trained. She might need to be the prey, the mouse who found a hole and burrowed in before the cat with claws could sink them into her. Or, in this case, the men with guns could riddle her with bullets. Her and Ethan. Mel hadn't lost a client yet. She wasn't about to do so now.

"We need to hide," she said. "Let them think we got away, maybe."

"Might work." Ethan glanced behind him, flashed a look at her vehicle, which stuck out from the mound of earth like a beacon—*here we are*.

They would have to leave it until she could hire someone to retrieve it.

It's just a car, she reminded herself.

"Let's go," she said.

They climbed around the mountain of dirt, keeping low, just short of crawling. Mel's feet sank ankle-deep in the soft earth. Her arms and legs shook. Too little to eat that day. Too little exercise these past few months.

"Once we're around," Ethan said with a little too much cheerfulness, "we'll be out of their—"

He didn't get to finish. Before the last word—*sight*, Mel presumed—was out of his mouth, a gunshot rang across the field.

Ethan dropped and rolled, trying to get out of range, away from gunfire, but into what? He didn't take the time to raise his head and look. Where they ended up didn't matter. They'd been spotted. He and Mel hadn't worked fast enough. Hadn't stayed low enough.

And thinking of Mel…

Ethan looked for her. She was nowhere in sight. She could still be behind him, stranded. Shot?

Ethan turned back, searching for her. Finally, he

spotted her white-blond hair. It stood out against the darker earth like a sunny flare. Not good. She needed a cap. She needed to move down his side of the man-made hill.

She was on her belly, looking back along the road. Ethan crept up beside her and followed the path of her sight.

The car had moved. It rested on the road below, two men crouched on the far side, one pointing a pistol with a barrel nearly as long as a rifle butt across the roof.

"Let's go," Ethan said. He didn't try to hide his exasperation. "We can't fight that."

"I'm thinking." Mel's voice was barely a murmur. "Do you think we can get them to follow us over here?"

"Why would we want—" Ethan broke off and looked behind them.

There was the hole that had once been filled with this mountain of dirt—a nicely squared-off pit. Fifteen feet square. Fifteen feet deep.

The lady was brilliant.

"I'll just show myself long enough to make them think they have a target…" Mel began.

Ethan resisted the urge to catch her shoulders and hold her in place. He had no right to touch her like that. At the same time, she couldn't be so careless with her safety.

"Better me than you," she said as though she understood his thoughts. "You have family."

Such sadness touched her voice, Ethan was almost glad he didn't have time to dwell on it, pursue why she had no family. He didn't need to know. They were comrades in arms for the moment only.

"We need to move fast," was all he said.

Before Ethan could stop her, Mel shot up her head so her pale hair blazed like a beacon against the dark dirt, then they let themselves roll down the hill, coming up hard and fast against the wooden barricade.

It barely held their combined weights. The boards shook and rattled upon impact. No problem with the noise. They wanted to be followed. Once they had purchase on the ground, though closer to the edge of the new foundation than Ethan liked, they kicked the boards loose, sending most of them into the basement with a tremendous crash of splintering wood. By the time they finished their destruction, their pursuers had reached the top of the mound. Ethan felt like a sitting duck on a precarious ledge. But the men's footholds weren't that sturdy, and their targets were moving.

A fourth shot reminded Ethan how risky their plan was. They might not reach cover fast enough. Cover might be flimsy at best. The men might not go rolling down the hill as he and Mel had.

A quick glance told Ethan his worst fears were realized. The men were moving upright, digging in their heels and holding out their arms for balance as though skiing on nothing but their shoe soles. The only good point was that they couldn't aim and fire while maintaining their balance.

He shouldn't look back. He needed to go forward.

He kept moving, but not before he realized the two men sliding down the hill weren't the same two who had accosted him the night before.

Derek had a lot of enemies and a lot of friends, apparently.

Ethan increased his speed, crawling after Mel, trying to plot out what would come next, how they would get away. In the men's car? Would they have left the keys?

Mel rounded the bottom of the oversized pile of dirt. Poor shelter indeed, if the men didn't fall. If they maintained their balance...

He didn't take time to consider that.

Mel was on her feet with Ethan following, running, running.

A shout and a cry told them one of their pursuers had fallen. One man. One shout of protest. A second bellow followed. The men were down. He and Mel were—

Not safe.

A third man blocked their path. Feet wide, face cold, Ethan's brother-in-law held a pistol pointed straight at Mel's chest.

FIVE

Never taking his eyes from his former brother-in-law, Ethan reached for Mel's hand. He probably should be diving for cover or thinking up a way to get out of this most recent jam. But his first thought was to hold on to Mel, to connect with her, have their hands united as their minds seemed to have been for the past hour.

She laced her fingers through his as though she, too, wanted contact with someone else. Comfort. Support. A reassurance neither of them was alone in what could easily end up their last moments on earth.

Once her long, slim fingers laced through his, Ethan experienced a rush of strength and peace. Death didn't scare him. He'd faced it enough to have made his peace with God. He hated the thought of leaving his family behind, of not being there to help and protect them, but if this was his time, then he would go and leave the rest in God's hands.

Calm now, Ethan was able to smile at the man who had once been a part of his family. Unwelcome, but still a member as long as he remained married to Sheila. "What brings you here?" Ethan posed the query as though they had encountered one another somewhere as mundane as a grocery store.

Except nothing to do with Derek was mundane. Everything from his wide-legged stance, his granite-hard face, to the Ruger gripped between both hands and pointed at Mel's chest, bespoke violence.

"You went to see my parents," Derek said. "Did you think they wouldn't tell me?"

Ethan shrugged. He knew that had not been a smart move even before Mel squeezed his hand nearly hard enough to hurt.

The lady was strong.

"Had to figure out how to find you." Ethan shifted his weight wholly to his right leg. "Figured they'd know where you were."

"Waste of time, wasn't it?" The merest taunt entered Derek's tone. "I wasn't about to bring them into this. I need their help raising the boys."

The boys. Ethan's nephews.

Was Derek saying that he was going to take the boys and give them to his parents? The elderly couple had never even met the boys. They hadn't reached out about staying in touch or being involved as grandparents once Derek had gone to jail, and Ethan certainly hadn't been about to offer.

It wasn't that they were bad people. They had always been perfectly polite to Ethan and the rest of the family. Yet Ethan couldn't help but wonder how they had produced a son like Derek. The way their son had gone wrong might have had nothing to do with his upbringing, but, on the other hand, their surface-level respectability might also be a cover-up for something... unpleasant.

No way would Ethan let those boys near Derek's parents. Or Derek.

He had to stay alive to protect the boys.

"No way will you have Sheila's boys," Ethan said with an effort to maintain his calm.

Mel rubbed her thumb on the back of his hand, and the calm returned—partially.

Derek's stiff features relaxed far enough for him to emit a humorless ha. "Don't see how you'll stop me."

Ethan had been afraid of this.

"You got the attention of those idiots you dropped into that hole," Derek continued, vocalizing Ethan's worst fears, "and I followed them."

"So they're not your men?" Ethan asked.

Derek snorted. "My men are more competent." He looked down at where Ethan and Mel were still holding hands. "Who is she?" He shifted the gun a little higher.

"She's…" Ethan hesitated. He didn't want to admit Mel was a PI.

"I'm his friend," Mel said.

Another jolt like being connected to a power outlet.

His friend. He liked that. He knew everyone in Mc-Clure, Kentucky. He liked most of them. He loved his family. But he didn't know anyone who would outright call him a friend and mean it in the way he suspected Mel did at that moment—friends beyond the casual get-together and playing a game of baseball or throwing some horseshoes. They'd known one another less than twenty-four hours, yet they had been through more than most acquaintances endured together in a lifetime. It was a special bond already.

"So where's my sister?" Ethan asked Derek.

The Rushmore cut of Derek's stony features cracked. "Used to be, I could never get her to shut up. But now, all of a sudden, she's decided to stop talking. Only reason why she's still alive. But we'll see how she sings once I have the boys. I'd thought of using you to force her cooperation, but…nah, I think it's time to take you out of the picture altogether before you make any more trouble. Then once you're gone, there'll be no one to stop me from taking back my boys."

Ethan's stomach rolled. "Over my dead body."

"That's the plan." The gun clicked.

Ethan threw himself in front of Mel, releasing her hand. "Run!" he shouted.

The gun blasted across the quiet construction site, and Mel was gone. Shot? Escaped? Ethan couldn't take the time to look.

Derek fired again. Once. Twice. Each time the bullets missed Ethan, who managed to dodge. But the quick, sudden start-and-stop movements were more than his knee could take. It buckled, and he fell to the ground. Fortunately, the timing meant that he fell right out of the path of another of Derek's shots.

How many more rounds? Ethan didn't remember. No matter. Killing only took one. He needed to get up, run.

His knee would not cooperate. Twice, he tried to rise. Twice, the already overtaxed joint collapsed beneath him.

And Derek was laughing. A deep belly laugh of amusement. "Can't get away. You're a sitting duck."

The trigger clicked. Nothing happened. Empty. The gun was empty.

Derek began to curse while reaching into his pocket for more bullets.

Ethan needed to go, find Mel.

Who was nowhere around. She wasn't lying on the hillside, bleeding. She wasn't taking evasive actions.

She was in the bad guys' car. It streaked down the road, sending up mud and gravel like confetti. Her face appeared fierce behind the windshield. Intense. Determined.

Ethan's middle roiled, but not with the same sense of dread he'd experienced moments earlier when Derek had mentioned getting hold of the boys. This was far more pleasant.

Derek spun at the roar of the engine. He must have managed to reload because he fired, but the bullet soared over the roof of the black Charger. When it became clear that he could either keep shooting or risk being mowed down, he began to run backward, trying to aim. The car kept coming. Forward... Forward...

Derek finally threw himself to the ground out of the car's path.

The Charger slowed, passenger's-side door popping open. "In," Mel commanded.

Ethan grabbed the swinging door and flung himself into the vehicle. Before he even got the door closed, Mel took off at full speed, fishtailing across the loose gravel on the construction site. One more shot followed them. It went wild, nowhere near their vehicle. Ethan latched the door, locked it.

"Good work," he said through gasps for air as they got back onto the road and sped away.

Mel said nothing. Lips set in a tight, thin line, she

kept her gaze flicking between road and rearview mirror, then back to the road.

"I'll keep watch." Ethan tipped the mirror enough for him to see what or who might follow. "You just stole a car." He hoped to make her relax.

"Borrowed."

"Derek's got a car too." He'd noticed it parked on the side of the road. But it was an inexpensive foreign model, something made for city maneuvering, not open-road speed.

"Four-cylinder piece of junk," Mel pronounced. "He'll never catch up with us."

"We're dead if he does."

Mel heaved an enormous sigh. "I thought we were dead back there. You got some good talking going there."

"Derek likes to brag."

The main road came into view, and Mel slowed.

"What do we do now?" Ethan asked. "Your car is…incapacitated."

"Yeah." Mel gulped. "We'll take this to the nearest Metro or L station and park it, then take the train back into the city. And in the meantime," she added, "we'll figure out our next steps in how to save your sister from that monster."

SIX

Mel shuddered at the idea of what Derek might do to Sheila to "persuade" her to give up the location of the money she had hidden.

"Derek is desperate." Ethan speared his fingers through his hair, making it fluff up into curls.

For a moment, Mel was distracted, wanting to smooth down the mussed hair to see if the thick waves were as soft as they looked. *Focus*, she commanded herself.

"They can't hurt her too much." Mel struggled to find something positive in the situation. "Not if they want her coherent enough to tell them anything they want to know."

"But it's not her pain they'll be using against her." Ethan gazed across the torn-up landscape. Looking at what, Mel couldn't tell. Maybe nothing he could actually see. "If she refuses to cooperate, they'll go for her children." Ethan's eyes were dark and hollow, as though he hadn't slept in a week. "He'll use those little guys like pawns on a chessboard."

"Kidnap them."

"Kidnap them," Ethan echoed.

She couldn't imagine the fear and the pain of knowing your nephews were about to become pawns in their father's game.

"So Derek could have recruited some guys to…" Mel hesitated.

"Go for my nephews?" Ethan supplied. "Makes sense."

Mel looked into Ethan's face. If she appeared half as bad as he did, she would give small children nightmares of zombies. A pallor had taken over the complexion beneath his tanned skin, tension rimmed his mouth and those hollow eyes. Not to mention the smears of dirt.

A good thing she didn't care much about her looks, especially in front of someone who was nothing more than a client.

Except she had never felt the impulse to smooth down the wavy hair of any other client.

Her stomach growling shook her from the thought. She didn't know when or what she had last eaten. Once they got back to the city, they should find somewhere to stop for a quick meal.

Neither spoke as they continued coasting down the highway. Talking seemed as though it would take more energy than Mel had. Ethan's silence proved he probably felt the same way. Or that he felt he had nothing to say that would be helpful. He didn't seem to be the sort of person who needed to fill quiet for the sake of filling quiet. Mel wholeheartedly approved.

Once they had traveled a few miles from the construction site, Mel pulled into a parking lot to look up the nearest train station on her phone. They were within walking distance of one, so they left the car in the parking lot and made their way past strip malls and filling stations to one of the furthest out L stations. In less than half an hour, they were seated side by side on a half-empty train headed for the city.

"I've never been on an L train before," Ethan admitted. "It's quite a view from up here."

"Not the best part of the city to see."

In truth, the train passed over neighborhoods known for multiple shootings a month and staggering poverty. The contrast between this and the area in which Mel's PI agency was headquartered never failed to distress her.

"The city gets prettier," she muttered.

"I like the view of the lake," Ethan said.

They changed trains in the Loop and stood on the platform gazing between buildings to the broad expanse of Lake Michigan, intensely blue beneath the sunny sky.

"It's like the ocean," Ethan said. "You can't see the other side."

Mel nodded. "You can see Indiana if you're high enough up, but not Michigan." She felt the vibration of an approaching train rattling through the wooden platform beneath her feet. "And in some ways, this is better than the ocean. The water isn't salty, and we don't have sharks or jellyfish."

Ethan chuckled, a low rumble like the wheels of the train on the aging tracks. "I admit I wouldn't go into the ocean."

The train stopped with a squeal of brakes, and the doors opened with a swish. They entered a car with no empty seats. Ethan grabbed an overhead strap to help maintain balance, but Mel was too short to reach one. When the train lurched forward, sending her half off balance, she grabbed for a pole or seat back for support. But a hand slid into hers, strong and steady.

Strong and steady like the man himself. All day he had been steady and strong. Calm. Thoughtful. Considerate. Even facing down a gun, he hadn't lost his cool. *Careful*, Mel reminded herself. *He's a client from Kentucky. He'll be gone in a day or two.*

Or less, if they managed to find his sister quickly.

"What do we do now?" she asked abruptly. "Do you still need my help? I mean... I can give you the address and directions to where I think your sister must be based on the numbers you got from her."

Ethan glanced around the car at the other passengers. They were engaged in reading newspapers, books, their phones. No one paid attention to anyone else. Mel doubted anyone could hear them above the rush of wind and the rattle of wheels. She still held his hand for steadiness, her shoulder occasionally bumping against his chest as they swayed around curves or jerked to a halt at stations.

"I still need your help." Ethan sighed, his breath stirring the hair above her ear. "Now that I know he's going to go after my nephews, it's even more important to me to get her away from Derek as soon as possible."

Mel didn't have a response to that other than, "We don't have enough time—not with how little we have to go on. We need more help on this. We need to go to the police."

"And what good will that do?" Ethan's tone held an edge of steel. "Even if we can convince them to take the case seriously, and can be certain that none of the cops working with us are secretly in Derek's pocket, what then? It's not like we know where to send them to find Sheila. At most, they could get a warrant to search Derek's house—but so what if they did? He'd never be careless enough to keep her there. We'd spend hours upon hours talking to officers and filing reports…all to be told at the end of the day that there's nothing they can do for us."

Mel couldn't argue with him, no matter how much she wanted to. The truth was, they were the best chance Sheila had—even if it felt like there was next to nothing that they could do.

"He will keep her alive until she talks," Mel said.

"And she'll talk fast if the boys are threatened," Ethan pointed out. "And then he'll kill her."

Ethan waited until they'd reached their station and returned to ground level before he told Mel what he was thinking, the decision he had made. "I need you to help Sheila get someplace safe after we free her."

"And how do we free her?"

"I'll offer myself as a substitute."

Mel was shaking her head in the negative before Ethan finished his sentence. "They have no reason to agree to that. If you turn yourself over, they'll just keep you both and make an example of you to get her to talk. You, now. The boys next."

"Derek would never kill his own kids."

"For half a million dollars?"

Mel's comment was harsh and direct, and all too true. Despite the warmth of the spring sunshine, Ethan shivered. Still, he pressed his point.

"I've already contacted my parents to warn them

that someone might be coming after the boys." He'd texted them from the car. "Maybe they'll be able to keep the twins safe and out of the hands of Derek's men. If Derek can't get the boys, he might grab the chance to have me to use against my sister. That would be enough to at least get us to where Sheila is, so you could break her out while Derek's busy with me."

"It's suicide, Ethan." Mel grasped his hands. Her fingers were as cold as he felt. "I can't allow you to do it."

"Do you have a better idea?" Despite knowing she was right, that he'd sign his own death warrant if he tried to trade himself for Sheila, Ethan challenged Mel to come up with a better solution.

"Not yet. I'm not trained in hostage negotiations. PIs don't get into that sort of thing." Her eyes shone suspiciously bright. "And I have nowhere to take Sheila."

"Your house?"

"Derek will be able to find me there. Looking people up these days is all too easy."

"Of course. Just because I'm not tied to my phone or the internet doesn't mean everyone else isn't when necessary."

"And not."

"And not." He managed a half smile.

"We probably shouldn't have come back here." Mel looked over her shoulder as though expecting someone to rush from the crowds on the sidewalk and grab her.

Grab her. He hadn't thought of that. Derek knew her now, had seen her face, had seen her with him. When the time came to tie up loose ends, Derek might come after her, to ensure she wouldn't be able to testify against him. Ethan had had no right to drag her into this mess. He should have had her give him the possible addresses and gone on his way.

Was it too late to do that now? Derek had seen her, but he didn't know her name, didn't know where to find her. Maybe she'd still be able to walk away if she left this case right now and Ethan handled it on his own from here. He was good at accomplishing feats on his own. He had been doing so all his life, from stopping a would-be bomber from destroying dozens of lives in Afghanistan, to turning the family's failing business into a prosperous enterprise. Protecting his family was, above everything else, his responsibility. It was what he'd committed his life to ever since coming home from overseas. He'd had no right to ask anyone to share that responsibility with him.

He would release Melissa Carter, PI, to go on about her business, and he would go on about his.

He released her hands and shoved his fingers into his pockets. "Go back to your office. I'll be fine on my own."

"Doing what?" Mel crossed her arms over her middle, chin lifted so she met his eyes.

Ethan opened his mouth to say the less she knew, the better, then decided to go for the truth. "I don't know yet."

"Then you need a plan." She caught hold of his elbow. "But first you need food. No one can think on an empty stomach."

"Mel—"

"No arguments right now." She tugged on his arm. He knew he should stand his ground—but it felt so good to have someone looking out for him that he found her caretaking hard to resist. He'd still send her away...but that could wait until they'd had a meal.

Without too much reluctance, he fell into step beside her, navigating through a clutch of people until they reached a café. Mel pushed inside and straight to a table away from the windows. Good instinct that. They didn't want to be obvious from the street in the event Derek or anyone else was looking for him.

"After this, I need to leave," Ethan said before an approaching server reached their table. "You can go back to your life and I'll—"

"Ethan!" Mel shouted his name as she surged to her feet. "The door."

Ethan swung around, standing at the same time. Two men pushed through the plate-glass door. Big men. Masked, armed men. Patrons screamed. Dishes crashed. Chairs toppled.

"Get down," Ethan called out.

He had no doubt these men were after him.

They should have gone to another part of town. They shouldn't have stopped for food. They should have—

No time for that. Time to run.

Mel grasped his hand and together they started toward the kitchen.

"Stop!" one of the intruders ordered.

They ignored him. A shot rang out. Harmlessly aimed high, to judge from the tinkle of a breaking glass light fixture. With so many people standing between Ethan and Mel, it would be difficult for the attackers to aim for them without someone else getting in the way.

He and Mel slammed through the swinging door into the kitchen. The room was empty of people. Pots of soup bubbled unattended on the burners. A timer buzzed, and smoke with the stench of burning bread and cheese filled the space.

Mel hesitated. "Where?"

"Outside."

"They'll have men posted there, don't you think?"

He agreed. Derek's guys wouldn't want anyone to go free and notify the authorities too soon.

No matter. Ethan and Mel had to break through those men before the others—

Too late. One of the masked men charged into the kitchen. Without thinking of the consequences, Ethan grabbed one of the pots of soup, scorching his palm on the handle, and threw it in the man's direction. Viscous fluid smelling of clam chowder slammed into the man's chest and mask. He yelled in what seemed to be a mixture of surprise and pain. They had a moment's advantage.

Mel had snatched another pot. Ethan grabbed a third. Imprecise weapons, but weapons nonetheless.

"Let's go," Ethan shouted.

Together, they blasted through the rear door, charged into the alleyway and the path of two more masked men.

Mel threw her entire pan full of tomato soup. It hit the man on the right, dripping down like blood. Ethan aimed higher, dousing the second man's head with chunks of chicken and long, fat noodles. The man shrieked and scrabbled at his mask.

But the first man lunged forward, aiming his gun straight at Mel. Ethan grabbed her, tried to haul her out of the path of the bullet. Impossible. No one moved faster than a bullet.

The man pulled the trigger. Ethan heard the click—but nothing happened. The gun, held steady in the man's hand, dripped with tomato soup as though it had been shot and lay across the man's fingers, bleeding out.

For a heartbeat, Mel and Ethan's eyes met. For a heartbeat, they allowed themselves a smile.

Then they ran.

The alley was narrow, made worse by trash receptacles and recycling bins lined against building walls on either side. At the far end, a recycling truck backed into the alley, its beep nearly drowning the shouts of the men chasing behind Ethan and Mel and the wail of an approaching siren.

The police were getting involved whether Ethan wanted it or not. Whether Derek wanted it or not. A foolish move on Derek's part, sending his goons in to attack Ethan and Mel in a restaurant full of patrons. He must know the cops would show up for such a display.

Ethan slid to a halt and drew Mel into a recess between a man-high trash bin and a doorway. He wasn't winded, but his bad knee refused to take any more pounding. If he continued, he would collapse.

Only when he faced a surprised-looking Mel did he realize he still held her hand. He released it at once. "Sorry."

"For what?" She leaned against the brick wall, hand to her heart.

Her breathing was a little elevated.

"Why would Derek want the cops involved?" Ethan asked, the question still circling in his mind.

"To delay us," Mel said without hesitation.

Ethan nodded. "That sounds plausible. But if he wanted to keep us from coming after Sheila, why strike in such a public place? I mean we were just getting a bite to eat. Wouldn't it have been easier to attack later, when there was no one else around? We wouldn't have been any closer to finding Sheila if he'd waited an hour."

"I...don't know." Mel ran a hand across her forehead. "Maybe he's working on a tight time frame. Doesn't matter. We need to get you away."

"Why don't you stay and talk to the cops. I'll go." Ethan wanted Mel safe inside a precinct; wanted her safe where the bad guys couldn't get hold of her.

"Not alone." Mel grasped his hand. Ethan tried to break her grip, but she was strong, determined.

"Mel, you're not safe if you stay with me."

"Tough." She peered around the dumpster.

Ethan followed her gaze from his height advantage. The alley appeared a chaos of people running, jostling, standing still—which were the invaders, he couldn't tell. At this point, no one wore a mask. Several were dressed in all black. The sun shone, so many wore dark glasses.

He and Mel needed to get out. Except the recycling truck still made its way down the alley, stopping every twenty feet to pick up a bin and dump its contents into the back.

"If we time it right, we can get past the truck when it's emptying a load," he said.

He said *we*, but he meant him. They would have to go single file past the truck. He would go first. She would have to wait for the next load to follow, by his calculations, and… He could lose her before she got past the vehicle.

But the woman was smart. When they reached the truck, she slipped ahead of him, shot him a grin over her shoulder, and snuck behind the recycling bin being raised to disgorge its load.

Ethan stumbled back to keep up with the truck. Saying a prayer for Mel's safety—and his own—he ducked to make the same maneuver as Mel.

The last thing he saw was a glimpse of her bright hair shining in a sliver of sunshine creeping between two buildings.

And then everything went black.

SEVEN

Mel skidded to a halt and glanced behind her. The truck had stopped. The wailing siren had stopped. Ethan was nowhere in sight.

Her stomach lurching, Mel sprinted back to where she had last seen him. Nothing. No one was there. She peered over the recycling bins and spied the crowd milling about the alley. A couple of cops had joined them, taking statements. For a moment, she was relieved. Ethan must have gotten waylaid.

Except she didn't see Ethan. With his height, he should stand out. But…no. He wasn't there.

Mel pressed her palm against the brick of the building, needing the solidity of cool, forged clay to steady her. She had lost Ethan. He could have ducked into a doorway, yet she didn't think so. He'd wanted to get away from the alley—from the cops and the assailants. So why hadn't he been right behind her?

She must be calm, think. He had to be all right. Just because she couldn't see him didn't mean he was in danger. Maybe the cops were questioning him somewhere out of her view. He could be in a patrol car or already on his way to a station. In any of those circumstances, he would be safe. Still, she needed to know where he was and verify his story.

She started to spin on her heel to race the rest of the way down the alley to the side street and around to where the cop cars were likely parked.

"That's her!" someone shouted.

"Miss! Police, stop!" The tone was brusque and authoritative.

Sighing, Mel turned, hands held at shoulder level. She wasn't armed, but they didn't know that. They weren't likely to shoot her, but she figured she shouldn't take the risk. "May I help you?" She faced a policeman and a man in a sanitation worker's uniform. Possibly the driver of the recycling truck.

"I need to ask you some questions, miss," the cop said.

"Of course." Mel smiled. Cooperation was the fastest way to get her free to look for Ethan.

"I understand you were with a gentleman the gunmen seemed to be targeting..." Mr. Officer began.

"I—" Mel began.

"Look," the man in sanitation uniform said, "with all respect and all, I need to get on with my route. Can you take this discussion elsewhere?"

Mel backed against the wall. "By all means."

Ethan, where are you, and how much should I say?

The officer moved against the wall, as well, as the recycling truck pulled away.

With egress from the alleyway free, Mel wondered if Ethan would appear. But she still couldn't spot him. While she was looking, the policeman stepped close to her and took her arm. "Let's go to my cruiser."

"All right." Mel sighed. No sense in arguing one

way or the other. She'd just have to answer the cop's questions first, and then she could text Ethan or try to find him. He couldn't be far.

The officer led Mel back through the restaurant to the street. A few tables sat on the sidewalk already, optimistic thinking on behalf of the restaurant, given that Chicago weather was potentially sunny and seventy degrees one day and snowing the next in early April. She had seen it happen. Nonetheless, she was grateful for the seats. Her knees were weak, her head light from a lack of nourishment on top of too much exertion. She should request water, at the least. Her mouth was as dry as a box of fresh newspapers. She licked her lips and swallowed, actions that probably made her look nervous and thus guilty. She was just thirsty.

"May I grab something to drink?" she asked.

Before the cop could answer, she darted back inside the restaurant, grabbed two glasses upside down on their tables, and filled them from pitchers of iced water on a waiter's serving cart. Topping each with a slice of lemon, she returned to the cop.

"Water?" She set a glass before him.

He raised a brow but thanked her.

Mel drank hers down in one long swallow. Once she set the glass on the table, she said, "Okay, I can talk now. You want my name, rank, and serial number?"

The cop allowed himself a half smile. "Something like that."

"I'm Melissa Carter. I'm twenty-seven, and I work at the O'Clare PI agency."

"In what capacity?" the cop asked.

Mel gave him a withering glare. "As a PI."

"Sure." He made a notation in his little notebook. "Your home address?"

Mel gave it to him, as well as her phone number. She also gave him Megan's information, so he could verify her employment or something, and pulled out her license to prove her official status as a PI in the state of Illinois. All of the information was entered into the officer's iPad.

"All right then." Seemingly satisfied with her bona fides, the officer began his true inquiry. "Why were you in the restaurant?"

"Lunch. I haven't eaten all day."

"Never a good idea." The cop glanced inside the little notebook. "Who were you with?"

In her head, Mel heard her friend Amber, a former employee of the agency, correcting the grammatical mistake—*With whom, Mel. With whom.*—before she laughed.

She suddenly missed Amber for no reason. She missed Megan and Jack. She missed Jessica and Karen, other agents. Most of all, she missed Ethan.

A scan of the three police cars lined along the curb told her he was neither in nor near any of them.

She shivered despite the warmth of the sun on her back.

"Tell me what happened," the cop prompted her.

"We sat down to order—"

"Who is 'we'?"

"I was with a client."

"Who is your client?"

Mel hesitated. "I don't think—"

"Miss Carter—" he leaned toward her across the table, wafting cinnamon-gum scent into her face

"—do not give me any client privilege nonsense. This is a serious criminal matter."

Arguing would only take up more time, and she still wanted to get this over with as fast as she could so she could concentrate on finding Ethan.

If he would let her find him.

For the first time, she considered that he might have managed to slip away from everyone; from the police, from the men after him…from her. As the danger to her had increased, she'd seen him grow more and more hesitant about her continuing in the investigation.

She sighed. "His name is Ethan McClure. He's from McClure, Kentucky."

"Why is someone from Kentucky hiring a Chicago PI?"

"He's looking for a missing person he believes is in this area."

"Who?"

"His sister," Mel answered.

"His sister." The cop's mouth thinned. "You sure about that?"

"Of course I'm sure about that. That's why he hired me."

"He hired you to find his sister, and in the process of looking for her, you get shot at by masked men?"

Bile surged into Mel's throat. It burned, and she coughed. It wasn't that she hadn't realized the situation was dangerous, but something about the cop stating it so bluntly really drove the message home.

Without a word, the cop picked up her water glass and carried it into the restaurant—for a refill, she supposed. He returned with a full glass.

She nodded her thanks and drank half the water in a single swallow. Cool liquid settled the rawness of anxiety in her throat and stomach.

"So where were we?" the cop asked, flipping the pages of his notebook.

Mel waited. She knew perfectly well he remembered where they had been before her coughing fit.

"Ah, yes." The officer nodded. "Hired to find his sister. Her name?"

"Sheila."

"McClure?"

"…Yes." It wasn't a lie—that was the name that Sheila was going by currently. Mel didn't want to bring up Derek's name if she could avoid it. Not when she knew how Ethan felt about getting the police involved. If there was any chance that dropping the wrong name would set Derek off and put Sheila in line for greater harm… No, Mel wouldn't take that risk.

"And had you made any progress in finding this… sister?" the cop asked.

"I think we're onto something," Mel admitted.

"And who was onto *you* and why?" he asked.

Mel hesitated between being a little smart-alecky or sounding naïve. She chose the former. "Bad guys."

The officer shot her a glare.

Mel shrugged. "Look, I don't know who they are, Officer, and I don't think I should tell you more without consulting my boss and possibly a lawyer. I have an obligation to my client to protect his information as much as the law allows. Since I've done nothing wrong, I don't understand this third degree."

"You've done nothing wrong?" The officer set down his iPad and looked straight into her eyes.

"Then why did we find your car half-buried at a construction site with bullet holes in the door panel?"

Ethan wasn't surprised to regain consciousness in the back of a van. His first thought was that he wished he was in the trunk of a car instead. He could have gotten himself out of a trunk. Vans, with doors that could be easily secured, were much more trouble to escape than trunks. But he supposed he was too big to fit into the trunk of most modern cars. As it was, the van was small, and he couldn't stretch out his legs. He was bent at hips and knees, and had been there long enough for the joints to ache, especially his bad knee. So the situation was pretty terrible on every level.

He should have been more careful. He'd known those men were after him. Yet he hadn't watched his back. Mel had been away from him for less than half a minute and—bang. They had been on him, knocking him out.

How they had carried him out of the alleyway without anyone realizing what they were doing, Ethan didn't know. He could, however, make some guesses about the excuses they could have used. He was a guest of the restaurant knocked down by people rushing from the premises. He wasn't well and had passed out. He hadn't eaten and hunger had overtaken him. Anything to get people to clear the way for them before the cops arrived.

And now they'd trussed him up like a chicken.

A zip tie secured his ankles. He figured another secured his wrists. He couldn't see those. They were pulled behind his back, the most awkward position when one wanted to get free.

So he would concentrate on his ankles.

Except, he couldn't reach his ankles with his hands. His right knee just wouldn't bend that far.

For a while, he lay still, listening. If two people rode in the van with him, they weren't talking. Either that or a soundproof barricade stood between him and the other passengers. There was no way to be sure when the cargo hold was pitch-black.

They had turned twice since he'd awoken, and the roads, though not level, were smoother than anything he had experienced in the country.

Being in the city made things easier. Help was more readily available among crowds of people— he hoped. In the city, he could learn fairly quickly whether Mel was all right or not. And his sister...

He must concentrate on getting himself free before he could think about Sheila. If he could make the zip tie stretch, he might be able to work it loose from his hand.

Two turns and a stop long enough to be a red light later, all he had accomplished was to cause cuts on his wrists. The zip tie remained as tight as ever.

He focused his attention on his ankles. Despite his knee, his legs were stronger than his arms, and they were not twisted behind him. He pressed his legs apart for ten seconds, held for ten, released. Repeat. Repeat.

Nothing.

He had begun to sweat. Zip ties apparently were not easy to break. Nor did they seem to stretch.

"Come on," he murmured.

A quarter inch more room was all he required.

Fortunately, he wore thick, cotton athletic socks, so his ankles weren't getting cut up like his wrists. He managed to kick off his shoes. Just the absence of the footgear made him feel freer, lighter. Removing the socks was more complicated. He had nothing with which to grab them and tug.

But the carpet in the van was new and stiff. By scraping his heels on the rug again and again, he managed to drag the socks down far enough so the knit lay lower than his ankles, lower than the zip tie. His right leg he managed to bend far enough so he could catch hold of the flapping toe of the sock with his bound fingers and yank it off.

He rolled onto his left side, but that right knee would not cooperate. Gritting his teeth from a pain in his back he'd never experienced before, he twisted and maneuvered, and managed to finally pull off his second sock. After that, removing his feet from the zip tie was simple.

If he got free now, he could run away. Okay, shuffle away.

If? It had to be *when*. And that "when" needed to be now.

He reached out with his toes to find where the van door opened in back—two doors that would swing in opposite directions. No lock or handles were apparent. The crack rose from floor to ceiling without a break. Latches must lie on the outside and out of his reach.

"Plan C or D." Ethan closed his eyes. Attempting to free his hands then removing his shoes and socks had worn him out, probably because he hadn't eaten or slept much in the past few days. No matter. He had to find reserves of strength and meet the men where he could. As soon as the van door opened, he would make his move.

As uncomfortable as lying on his bound hands

proved to be, Ethan did it anyway, his feet raised and ready for movement outside the van's back door.

The van slowed, stopped, turned. It sped up again. The brakes slammed, jerking the vehicle forward then back.

The van made an abrupt turn and began to reverse up an incline. A driveway? That could be good or not. Driveways meant houses. Houses potentially meant people—Sheila, Mel.

Not Mel. Please, not Mel. He didn't want to think of her being captured.

Regardless of where they were now or who was there, someone was likely to open the van to remove him. They'd chosen to capture rather than kill him. That meant they still wanted him for something.

Ethan braced himself. The van opened. A rush of cool air swept into the cargo hold.

And Ethan launched himself out, feet planted in the center of one bad guy's chest.

EIGHT

Mel thought the cops would never let her go. By the time the first one finished questioning her, a detective had shown up and began questioning her all over again. Though she was distracted with worry for Ethan, her answers never changed. They couldn't. She told the truth. She told more of the truth than she was comfortable telling regarding a client's business.

The last time she had divulged a client's personal business was when the ex-husband had stormed the agency office. She hadn't been any more comfortable then than she was now. Ethan wouldn't like it. But Mel needed their help finding him.

Or maybe not finding him. She was fairly certain she knew the location of Ethan's sister, and now, she feared, him. It was where they'd been headed when they'd been chased down by that black Charger that had forced them to wreck. Mel hadn't been willing to continue driving all the way there in a stolen car, but she'd thought that once they'd gotten back into the city and figured out some other means of transport, she and Ethan would go together. But if Ethan had been captured, then he might have been dragged there without her.

It was a town to the southwest, a fairly affluent community of people who commuted into the city during the week and enjoyed a peaceful lifestyle at home. The sort of town thought a good place for raising children.

And yet a drug dealer was using that town, using one of the fine homes there, for his headquarters. He was holding his ex-wife there, hurting and terrorizing her. He was planning to bring children there to hurt and frighten them as well.

Mel had to get there as fast as she could, and she couldn't go alone.

During one of the short breaks the police allowed her between inquisition sessions, she texted her boss with an SOS. By the time Mel was allowed to go, Megan and Jack had pulled up to the curb in an unobtrusive gray Honda.

"You've got a lot of explaining to do, Melissa Anne Carter," Megan said in her best "mom" voice, though they were practically the same age.

Megan was dressed in a calf-length green skirt and matching print blouse. Her feet were shod in medium-heeled pumps. Jack wore slacks and a button-down shirt. Dress-up clothes.

"What wedding festivities did I drag you away from?" Mel slid into the back seat, feeling like a ragamuffin in her dirty, rumpled jeans.

"Lunch with the wedding planner." Megan grimaced.

"She's trying to talk us into eloping," Jack said, grinning.

Megan punched his arm. "*You're* the one trying to talk me into eloping, even if you're going to look amazing in your tux."

The tips of his ears grew pink, and he caught Mel's eye in the rearview mirror. "Talk. I've heard more than enough of weddings."

"You know about my client, Ethan McClure," Mel began.

"The one I told you sounded tricky? Seems to me like I also said that you should be on your guard or you might end up in danger, right?" Megan clarified.

Mel ducked her head. She knew she'd been taking risks with this case. And yet...

The feel of his warm, strong hand on hers sent something quivering inside her middle, and she couldn't regret putting herself at risk to help him. She wouldn't have gotten to know him. She wasn't used to letting people in, was still uncertain about it, but something about Ethan made her want to try.

She gave her head a vigorous shake. "Okay, you can say 'I told you so,' and it won't change any of this. We've got one woman already being held captive, possibly being tortured to make her talk. We have my client, who has gone missing and might have been kidnapped so that he can be used to put pressure on his sister. And we have a pair of twin boys back in Kentucky who are at risk of being taken as leverage too. I can't just ignore all of that, even if it means I'm putting myself at risk."

"Okay," Megan said, her expression serious. "Start from the top. We're listening."

Mel leaned forward between the front seats as far as her seat belt allowed and began to talk. She gave them as many details as she could beyond the hand-holding and the way looking into his eyes kicked up her heartbeat.

Megan and Jack, well trained in listening, said little beyond asking a few questions for clarification over locations, distances, number of people present. In short order, they'd arrived at the office, where Megan immediately sat at her computer and started inputting data.

"If he's such a big guy," Megan asked when Mel sat back and sipped at the water she'd grabbed from the kitchen, "how did he just disappear from the alley behind the restaurant?"

"Good question," Mel answered. "They must have knocked him out so fast he didn't know it was coming. And then they just tossed away their masks from earlier, turned into regular guys, and carried him off like he was sick or something."

Megan looked away from her screen to pin Mel with a penetrating stare. "He doesn't sound like the kind of guy who would have gone down without a fight—unless he was distracted. Was he paying more attention to you?"

"He might have been making sure I got to the other side of the recycling truck safely." Mel tried to keep her tone even, though a stab of guilt pierced through her heart.

"Uh-huh." Megan's full lips, wearing gloss for once, pressed together in a grim line. "Attractive, is he?"

Mel shrugged. "I guess so. I mean if you like the all-American country-boy type."

"Very attractive," Megan concluded.

"Hey," Jack protested. "What about the all-American city-boy type?"

"Even more attractive." Megan bestowed a smile on him so tender, so loving, tears pricked Mel's eyelids.

Mel tried to avoid the tidal wave of envy washing over her—and failed. She had prayed for a family for years. She'd lost her mother when she'd been almost too young to even remember her, and while she'd loved her father, she'd been painfully aware of how small and fragile their little family was. And then she'd lost her dad too.

She had found a sort of family in the ladies of the agency. Yet Megan was getting married, Jessica and Karen were constantly on assignment somewhere and rarely free to get together to socialize, and Amber was off to Pittsburgh for the foreseeable future. At night when she went home, Mel returned to an empty house. Sometimes her cat was around, but Mel was gone so much she had installed a pet door so the cat could visit a neighbor lady she adored. The feline didn't like to be alone for long, so she was often gone when Mel arrived home.

"So what do you want us to do?" Jack asked, yanking Mel from her moments of self-pity.

She had no business feeling sorry for herself when Ethan and his sister and probably his nephews were in danger.

"We've got to free him," Mel said. "I'm afraid they'll do something like hurt him in front of his sister to get her to talk."

"Why doesn't she talk?" Megan asked.

"Because she's dead as soon as Derek gets what he wants. I've looked this man in the eye—I can tell you with absolute certainty that he'd have no qualms about killing someone, even the mother of his children. Maybe *especially* the mother of his children— after all, she stole from him and she's the reason why he went to jail. The only reason she's still alive is that he wants that money back."

"But why keep the money in the first place?" asked Jack, the forensic accountant. "Didn't she know it would paint a target on her back?"

"Maybe she thought she could use it as a bargaining chip if he came back," Mel said. "If so, that definitely backfired on her."

"Or maybe she wanted the money for herself," Jack pointed out.

"I don't think…" Mel couldn't continue. She didn't want to think Ethan's sister was trying to find a way to keep the ill-gotten money. And yet…

"Why else wouldn't she tell the cops where it is?" Megan voiced Mel's sudden apprehension.

"I don't think—" Mel said again.

And again, she stopped.

She wasn't thinking through everything, asking all the questions a good private investigator should. She had taken Ethan's word for everything right from the start.

Yet why not? She was generally a good judge of character, and his character seemed stellar. Yet she didn't know his sister, and maybe he didn't either. People saw what they wanted to, believed what they wanted to, of those they loved.

Mel couldn't discount the fact that Sheila had been involved with Derek enough to marry him and bear him two children. She had known about the drug selling and had taken time to report him. Of course, she had needed to get several things in place to do so, but still…she'd taken the money in the end. Even as she'd worked with the police to uncover the drugs, to charge him with possession and assault, she'd held something back. Half a million somethings.

As much as Mel wanted to trust both McClures, those questions held her wary of a full commitment to believe every word—again.

Had she really not been thinking of the practical, the crucial, when with him? No, she hadn't. Something about him had drawn her in, made her trust, even when her past most certainly should have taught her better.

No wonder all the detectives in mystery novels were single. Attraction between human beings was far too distracting for good concentration on one's work.

"But it doesn't matter." Mel spoke up as though she had been talking all along. "We are still going to rescue him."

"Do you have a plan?" Jack asked.

"Um, not really." Mel rubbed her eyes. "I guess we should do some recon. I mean I'm pretty sure about the address, but I haven't actually gone to check it out myself."

"That should happen tonight," Megan said. "We've got a thing with my mom, but then after that, the three of us can drive out and get the lay of the land. See if Derek's really using it as his headquarters. Figure out how many people he has with him. Check for any signs to confirm that Sheila and/or Ethan is there. And then we—" Whatever she was going to say next was cut off by a huge yawn. "Sorry, sorry," she apologized. "Long day again. And I guess tomorrow will be even longer, once we've gathered enough intel to put together a plan of—" Another yawn interrupted her, but she stifled it long enough to finish saying, "Attack."

"What you need is a good night's sleep," Mel said. "Especially if you're going to be in fighting shape tomorrow. I can do the recon on my own. We can meet back here in the morning and I'll let you know what information I was able to gather."

Megan seemed like she was going to protest, but after exchanging a look with Jack, she sighed and nodded her agreement.

"Oh, but there is one thing…" Mel said, a little embarrassed. "Can I borrow a car?"

Ethan's heel landed on the man's chin. The blow would have been more effective had Ethan been wearing shoes or boots. Nonetheless, the man staggered backward, landing against the aluminum garage door with a boom like thunder.

Ethan managed to stand, grasping the edge of the cargo hold floor with his bound hands, feet landing on the cold concrete floor of the garage they had pulled into. He had seconds to free himself. Seconds to get out of a space where any number of other men might appear at any moment wielding guns or other weapons, and snapping on more zip ties.

An exit. He needed a quick exit. There, beside the garage's main sliding door, the oblong of a smaller, secondary door, its window covered. The man Ethan had kicked in the jaw was rising on his feet to his full height between Ethan and that door.

The man wore a gun. Its outline wasn't in the least disguised beneath his jacket. Ethan's only advantage was that the man hadn't yet palmed that gun. He'd been confident that his prisoner was too trussed up to fight.

Or he had backup.

Of course he had backup. Ethan had yet to see any of these men operate solo, except for Derek himself.

"Stay. Where. You. Are." The man gave the command between gasps for air and through a swelling jaw.

Ethan took a step toward that outside door. "I don't like your hospitality."

The man reached for his gun. "Don't. Move."

Ethan took another step toward the door. "You won't shoot me. I'm no good to you dead."

"You'll be plenty good to us with one bullet in you." Another voice spoke from around the side of the van. "To start."

Of course he would. A wounded arm, a grazed side, would show Sheila they meant business when they told her they would hurt him even more if she didn't spill the beans.

Ethan leaned against the van, his bound hands seeking something he might be able to yank loose and use as a weapon. A tire iron wouldn't normally be much good against a gun, but it could be effective in these close quarters. If the area for storing equipment was beneath the floor of the van's cargo hold, accessible with the rear hatch open, he might be able to reach inside, bound hands or not.

He groped behind him for a latch. "Will your neighbors think gunshots are all right in the middle of the afternoon?"

"Ever heard of a silencer, country boy?" The man around the side of the van practically sneered the words. "Now step over here and don't do anything stupid again."

Not yet. He had discovered a latch.

"I'm not sure I'll like my accommodations." Ethan smiled to make the words sound flippant, unconcerned.

He flipped the latch. Speaking of gunshots, the click the release made seemed as loud as one.

But maybe that was just to him. The men didn't react.

"Get moving." The first man made no secret of his exasperation. "Or better yet, don't. I want an excuse to make your jaw look like mine feels." He fingered the swollen flesh.

It would look worse if Ethan could get hold of... something.

He tried to slip his hands inside the compartment. No go. He had to lean back. The position was awkward, throwing him off balance. Yet he tried. This was his best chance.

"Move it." The first man kicked Ethan's left knee.

He gasped and stiffened his leg in an effort not to collapse from the surge of pain. Despite the absence of shoes, he swung a kick at the man, aiming high for his middle. The man darted away, and Ethan lost his balance and fell backward into the van. As he fell, his hands slipped into the hidden compartment. One hand curled around something cold and metallic. In a flash, he pulled it free, jumping out of the van and spinning on a bare heel, turning his back to the men so that he could aim the weapon in the hands that were still bound behind him. He had little more chance of striking either of the men effectively than a blind man hitting a moving target with an arrow. But it might encourage them to stand back to avoid being struck. This might give him a few seconds of advantage.

A few seconds was all he needed.

He began swinging the tire iron behind him, striking the side of the van, the garage door, something neither metallic nor concrete. The men shouted at him, sounding panicked, or maybe just annoyed, warning him to stop or they'd shoot. He knew they were likely to follow through on their threats. Every second on his course to the door, he imagined the boom of a pistol, the burn of a bullet tearing through flesh, him stumbling, maybe falling, definitely bleeding.

They didn't shoot. Maybe they were lying about having silencers. All he knew for sure was that he'd ended up at the door.

A door he had to unlock before he could turn the handle—which required dropping his weapon.

He turned his back to the door. The tire iron slipped to the concrete floor with a clang, the sound magnified in the enclosed room. Now he could see both men, though not the face of the second man. He kept his mask on as he raised his gun to take aim.

Ethan's searching fingers found the lock, fumbled it open, then closed around the door handle. It pressed down, but the latch didn't disengage.

The armed man drew back his trigger with a decisive click.

Ethan shoved the door handle up this time. The latch popped, and he yanked the door open, eyes still locked on the pistol that fired at him the instant he grabbed the edge of the door and spun into sunshine and fresh air.

NINE

Mel heard the echoing boom of a gunshot through the car windows from a quarter block away. She had arrived close enough to observe the house at the address her research had uncovered. She'd seen the van when it arrived. Some instinct had told her that she should intervene, that Ethan was inside...but she'd held herself back. There was no reason to think Ethan was in the van. He'd been taken hours earlier—whatever transport had brought him to the house should have arrived ages ago.

But what if they took a circular route to avoid being followed? she found herself thinking. It was certainly a possibility...but it was just a theory. That's why she had come to do recon—to try to gather some facts. *But what if he's hurt?* she thought next. She pushed that fear aside as well. She couldn't just go charging in, riled up and unprepared. That wouldn't do anyone any good.

Then the gunshot blasted at the same time the garage side door opened. And Ethan was there, bent forward at an odd angle, his frontward movement more a fast shuffle than a run.

Not that anyone could outrun a bullet.

Another shot rang out. Ethan dropped.

With shaking hands, Mel dialed 9-1-1. As succinctly as possible, she described what she was seeing and begged for someone to come quickly.

She couldn't tear her eyes off Ethan; couldn't even blink. He lay facedown in the driveway. Now she saw that his hands had been trussed behind his back.

The man had gotten free, or almost free, with his hands tied behind his back. And he was barefoot. Really? They had taken his shoes?

Two men stepped from the garage, glancing around as though afraid their gunshots had attracted undue attention. Not surprisingly, they hadn't. The nearest house was a thousand feet away and appeared unoccupied. A For Sale sign stood in the yard, shiny and new.

The men's gazes roamed along the street, the empty open land beyond, and returned. They spotted the car. *Busted.* There was no way for her to continue hiding. Her only choices were to stay and try to help Ethan or to drive away immediately.

Well, there was really only one option. No way was she leaving Ethan behind.

Diving out of the car, she sprinted up the driveway toward Ethan and the two men. They seemed too startled at the sight of her sudden charge to react right away, and she used that against them. Diving for one of the men, she used all the momentum she could muster to knock him to the ground.

He scrambled for his gun, but she got there first, snatching it out of its holster. Her stomach turned just at the feel of the weapon in her hand, but she swallowed down the bile and used it as a club, knocking out the man she was grappling with.

Rising fluidly to her feet, she aimed the gun at the other man. The one who was standing over Ethan, a foot on his back to hold him down and a gun aimed at his head.

"Step away from him." She gave the man an order she didn't expect him to obey.

As presumed, he didn't obey her order. Instead, he adjusted the placement of his foot on Ethan's back and pressed down. Ethan grunted.

Mel struggled for self-control as she glared at the man. "Your friend's down and the police are on their way. Do you think they'll let you go?"

"They can try to take me," he said with a shrug, sounding unconcerned. "But they'll have company faster than they can tie me up."

Mel barely stopped herself from asking, "Company?" Because she knew the answer.

These men had just arrived. If Derek was holding Sheila at this address, she wasn't alone. Why the other men hadn't come outside yet, Mel didn't know, but she could guess.

They didn't dare leave Sheila without a guard. These men were supposed to take care of themselves and their hostage unless commanded otherwise.

Mel shrugged. "Stalemate, I guess. We'll just have to stand here and wait until the cops come."

The man laughed. "When will they be here?"

"Soon."

Not soon enough.

Mel strained her ears, wishing for a siren, but none came.

"Should just walk away while you still have the chance, blondie," the man snarled. "If you stick around, this ain't gonna end well for you—for any of you."

For a moment, she wanted to lie on the driveway with Ethan and surrender. She was tired—tired of fighting, tired of running, tired of putting herself in danger for a man who was still a stranger and a woman who seemed to be playing some kind of dangerous game.

Then Ethan spoke one word from his prone position. "Boys."

Boys. His nephews. If they didn't get Sheila free of her former husband, two little boys would suffer at the hands of their father. They needed to grow up safe and secure with a strong, honest male influence in their lives, not a drug-dealing, murderous felon.

Mel straightened to her full height, little though it was in comparison to the man in front of her, and looked Derek's goon in the eye. "Then you'd better take me prisoner too."

"No, Mel." Ethan heaved his back against the foot pressing down. "Go. Run. The cops—"

"Will find nothing when they get here," the man sneered. "If they get here. We're not in the city, you know."

Mel wanted to kick herself for not thinking of another barricade to the police working quickly. This far outside of the city, police forces were much smaller, much slower to respond to an emergency.

And the man had just implied they were going to move Sheila and now Ethan. This location was the only lead she had. If she walked away and the others left, would she ever be able to find them again?

"Walk away," Ethan said.

She should take his advice. She should run back to safety, let the cops take care of the rest.

Yet the move could mean losing them. The move could mean Derek was taking his operation to Kentucky

and his boys. Without more information to go on to help
her track them, her only chance of helping was from
within, as a prisoner.

She dropped to her knees beside Ethan, tossing the
gun off to the side. "I'm staying here."

Ethan closed his eyes, even though he could see
little beyond the gray concrete beneath him. He didn't
want to even risk seeing what happened to Mel. This
wasn't the first time she had taken a risk to spare him.
What had she said when they were at the construction
site? He had a family; she didn't.

Did the lady think she could save the world? Or
that she should just because she didn't have a family?

"Do what I say," the man said to Mel, "or I'll blow
him away."

Faster way to go than as a pawn for Derek to force
Sheila to talk.

But Mel would obey. If she stayed, she wouldn't
risk Ethan's life.

An odd heat burned in Ethan's eyes—burned
straight through to his heart. He had spent so much
of his life caring for other people, he felt overwhelmed
by others, by strangers, caring like this for him and
a sister they had never met. His sister and nephews.

"Now you get up," the man said to Ethan next,
nudging him in the ribs with the toe of his boot. "And
don't you move, lady."

"It's Mel." She almost sounded like she was smil-
ing. "I prefer my name to *lady*."

The man said nothing. Ethan half smiled. She was
either brave, or delirious, or deliriously brave. She
couldn't be as calm as she pretended. Ethan's heart
was pounding, and he had seen combat. But his sur-

vival had never seemed as precarious as it did now. And not just his survival. His sister's. Mel's.

He never should have brought her into this.

Too late now. They were too deeply involved to go back to anything safe. They could only move forward and work for the best. Pray for the best.

With difficulty, Ethan struggled first to his knees and then to his feet. His right knee felt as though someone had taken a blowtorch to the joint, his shoulders didn't feel much better.

"You go first." The man waved his gun at Mel. "Inside."

Mel walked forward, hands tucked into the pockets of her jeans. The man marched Ethan behind her. They entered the garage where they were met by another armed man. Ethan had hoped they would enter the house where Sheila was held captive. Instead, they were directed to the van.

"Get in," the gunman who'd just joined them commanded.

Mel climbed into the cargo bay as the man gripping Ethan shoved him in face-first. His head struck something hard. Mel's knee. He grunted.

"Be gentle with him," Mel said. "He's a wounded veteran."

The two men laughed as though she'd made a joke.

And Ethan decided to pretend he was worse off than he was. Instead of helping himself move further into the cargo hold, he went limp. Perhaps they would think he had knocked himself out and not secure his ankles again. Without shoes and socks, getting out of ankle restraints wouldn't be as easy as it had been the first time.

With many grunts of effort, the two men shoved

Ethan the rest of the way into the van, rolling him onto his back. Lying on his hands would do him no good. His arms were likely to go numb. Having his arms behind him strained his shoulders, shooting pain up his neck and into his head.

He didn't need a headache. He needed to be able to think clearly, to plan, to figure out a way to get Mel out of this situation.

"Hands out—I need to secure you," one of the men commanded.

"If you must." Mel sounded resigned, not frightened.

Ethan turned his head and saw her hold her hands out before her. Blessedly smart lady. An old trick. If one played cooperative and held one's arms out in front, the captor would usually secure the hands that way rather than insisting on having them behind her back.

They zip-tied her hands then her ankles. She sat propped against the side of the van, eyes closed as though she was ignoring what they were doing to her.

Without another word, someone slammed the hatch closed.

"What now?" Mel asked.

"Can you help me roll onto my side?" Ethan asked, face heating. "My arms are going numb."

"Yes."

She grasped his shoulder. "Were you shot? Are you injured?"

"Just my pride."

Ethan pressed his hands down as hard as he could to assist Mel in rolling him onto his side. They hadn't resecured his ankles.

"I'm sorry," he said.

"For what?" Mel had left her hand on his shoulder. She peered down at him, her face nothing more than a pale blur in the near total darkness.

"For you getting into this." He sighed to ease tightness in his chest. "I've not only failed to save my sister and probably my nephews, too, but I've also put you in serious danger."

Mel squeezed his shoulder between her bound hands. "I couldn't leave you on your own. We'll get out of this."

He smiled. "I like your faith."

"It's all that's gotten me through these past few years."

For a moment, they said nothing. Ethan listened for hints of what was going on outside the van, inside the house. A couple of thuds, a shout, were all that penetrated the walls of the cargo hold. Then silence.

"We should be careful what we say," Mel said. "Someone could be outside the van listening. Or they could have listening devices inside here."

"Of course."

That made making plans of any kind difficult.

"They're going to take us somewhere," Ethan said. "It might be—" he swallowed "—to kill us."

"Yes, there's a big lake out there and lots of woods north in Wisconsin." Mel's tone was as even as Ethan had tried to make his.

"Then they'll go after my nephews," Ethan continued.

Mel leaned forward and murmured in his ear so softly he barely heard her. "Then we have to get ourselves out of this predicament, don't we? Let's concentrate on that and not on how bad things are right now."

Ethan tilted his head so his cheek brushed hers for

the merest moment. Acknowledgment of the sense of her words. Acknowledgment of them being a team. Acknowledgment that they might not succeed, but they would try their hardest.

Then Mel straightened so she leaned against the wall again. "I hope it's a long ride. I could use a nap."

Ethan's eyebrows climbed his forehead. He imagined she was playing for any potential listeners, but maybe there was a thread of truth to it too. He was also tired, worn down from stress and lack of sleep and anxiety for his family and now Mel.

"Not a bad idea to get some sleep," he decided to say. "I haven't—"

A scream interrupted him—a scream he recognized. Sheila.

Shouting followed. Male voices followed by the crash of breaking glass. A window. Nothing less would make that much noise. More cries from Sheila, then from a man, then an eerie silence.

They had done something to his sister. She was hurt or worse, and he was helpless to go to her aid. Everything he and Mel had been through for nothing.

He struggled against his bound hands, tried to sit up. He pounded his bare feet against the van's hatch.

The third time he struck it, it popped open, not from his blows, but from someone releasing the lock. Light flooded the cargo hold. Ethan blinked against the glare. Before he adjusted to the brightness, a form was tossed into the van like a discarded rag doll.

But this was no doll. This was his sister, limp and unconscious. *Only* unconscious, he hoped.

TEN

Before the door of the cargo hold slammed, leaving them in near total darkness again, Mel caught a glimpse of the woman who had been tossed into the van with such carelessness. She had a bruise growing over one temple. Other than that, her face was downright beautiful amid a spill of tangled golden-brown hair. Her figure was petite, even smaller than Mel herself.

Ethan's gasp of "Sheila" told Mel this was his sister, which came as a surprise. They looked nothing alike. Sheila was so small to his largeness, and her features were delicate, a violet next to an oak.

And now the three of them were crammed together in the back of a van, all three with bound wrists, two with bound ankles. One of them was unconscious. The other two were worn out from chasing and seeking and fighting all day and some the night before.

If only the cops would get here now.

They did not come within the minutes the men took to open the garage door and back the van onto the driveway, then the street. The minute the vehicle's tires hit blacktop, the driver hit the gas. Mel fell forward over Sheila, who made no sound or other indication she felt the impact.

Mel pushed herself to a sitting position again and found something hard beneath her right hip. After twisting a little, she was able to get her hands on it and identify it as a shoe. A large, man's shoe.

"I found your shoe," she said.

It was inane under the circumstances, but thinking seemed impossible at that moment. The van careened around first one corner, then another. Mel, Ethan, and Sheila flopped about like puppets with broken strings. When the driver slammed on the brakes, they slid forward, pretty much helpless to stop themselves. When the driver hit the gas again, they slid back. If the lock on the hatch broke under their combined weight, they would all spill onto the pavement like broken furniture off a moving van. Mel figured she would be a mass of bruises by the end of the ride.

But at that point, bruises might not matter. She might be dead.

Once she heard a siren nearby and hope rose. But it sailed past in the opposite direction. The van didn't matter to them.

Finally, after five more turns followed by a long straightaway, Mel managed to say, "Why aren't the cops pursuing us?"

"What would they pursue?" Ethan responded. "When you called 9-1-1, you just told them the address, right? You didn't mention the van."

When Mel stopped to think about it, she realized that the police might not end up investigating at all. The house was empty, after all. From the sounds of glass breaking, it did seem like there would be visible signs of a struggle left behind—but with no one to question and no idea of who was involved, there was a limit to how much the police could do other than questioning the name on the county property owner records. If that person was Derek or one of his cohort, they would deny knowledge of anything untoward. They certainly would have no reason to try to track down vehicles.

Mel closed her eyes and leaned her head against the padded side of the cargo hold. She needed to figure something out or this would probably be her last ride to anywhere. Sheila had information Derek wanted. Ethan was a means by which the men could persuade Sheila to give up her knowledge. But Mel... Mel was nothing more than a loose end to be tied up.

In most cases, PIs are nothing but a liability. The memory of those words from Edith—her father's longtime partner on the force—shot straight from Mel's brain to her heart, cracking it open and giving it a few kicks. She remembered the horror and disgust on the face of her godmother.

Mel had just told her dad and Edith that she intended to become a private investigator in an all-female agency instead of continuing on to become a police officer. Her father had been hurt. Her godmother livid.

Most cops held PIs in low esteem. From their perspective, private investigators messed up crime scenes and intimidated witnesses.

You'll be nothing but a drain on society.

Right now, Mel believed her godmother. If she couldn't do better by her client, she was worse than useless.

I will save him. Them. She made the vow as she realized Ethan was talking to her.

"I'm sorry?" she said.

"Will you check on Sheila?" He sounded oddly breathless.

"Sure."

She should have done so sooner. She tried to make up for the delay now, using her bound hands to locate first Sheila's head then her face. The bump on her temple seemed to have grown to the size of an avocado, but it wasn't bleeding. Mel found no signs of blood. Around Sheila's wrists, scabs suggested she had struggled against restraints. The current zip ties had broken some of those scabs open, making her skin sticky, but the cuts didn't seem to be bleeding very heavily.

Mel started to move on, then returned to the zip tie. They were pretty much impossible for the person wearing them to remove. But for someone else, unhooking them was not impossible.

"I'm going—" She stopped herself.

If a microphone was hidden somewhere in the cargo hold of the van, she didn't want to give away that they were attempting an escape from their bindings.

"I'm going to look her all over," she said instead. "Make sure no bones are broken."

She actually did check—and was relieved to note that everything seemed fine except for the fact Sheila was far too thin for good health. Considering she'd been taken less than a week ago, her thinness couldn't all be blamed on her captivity. Mel wanted to ask Ethan if his sister was in poor health. She couldn't believe he wouldn't notice his sister's skin and bones state.

"She seems all right," Mel told Ethan. "She's kind of thin."

Ethan sighed. "I know."

He didn't elaborate and Mel didn't press. If he didn't want to tell her, Sheila's condition was none of her business, no matter how curious she might be.

She returned her concentration to Sheila's hands first. If only Mel had fingernails. She recalled biting them to the quick while being questioned by the police. Ugh. It was a bad habit she thought she'd broken. Now she had little with which to work the clip that secured the tie. But she kept at it, bending, twisting, poking at the stiff plastic band. She had taken these things apart before. She could do it again.

"Is something wrong?" Ethan asked, then emitted a huff of a laugh. "I mean other than us being bound up back here going to...wherever?"

"I think everything is as good as it can be." Mel bent the clip on the tie in one direction, then the other. She gritted her teeth so hard her jaw ached. She knew there was a trick to the release. She had to lift the clip one way, twist the tail with the holes in it? No, *lift*. The clip slid free. The tie fell away from Sheila's wrists. Mel barely stopped herself from a cry of triumph as she scrambled for it and tried to slip it into her pocket. No good. She couldn't reach. She shoved it into her waistband instead and hoped it didn't fall through. Zip ties were just too convenient to have around.

"Mel?" Ethan sounded tense. "What—"

Mel managed to press her finger across his lips, signaling him to stop talking. His lips felt dry, a little chapped. He probably hadn't had water in hours. None-theless, they felt like nice lips. Soft beneath the dry-ness. If he weren't a client and if she weren't so wary about romantic entanglements, she might—

She jerked her mind away from such thoughts. She hadn't kissed anyone since she had caught her fiancé cheating. She'd thought she had found someone she could trust, someone she could build a life with—and she'd been wrong. When she'd caught him, he hadn't even taken responsibility or offered to try to work through their problems. He'd just said that it was her fault for never being around, given her un-predictable work hours, especially all the late nights she'd spent working.

She had taken all the hard nighttime cases then. Being alone in her house during the day didn't bother her so much as being alone there at night, especially in the months following her father's death. But rather than offering comfort or understanding, her former fiancé had just used it as an excuse to sleep around. She was definitely better off without him in her life… but the breakup had left her lonelier than ever. That must be the only reason why she would think about kissing Ethan McClure.

She knew better than to open up her heart—and risk having it broken again. What she needed to do was keep her mind on what was important—freedom.

She began to creep toward the front of the hold, the only way to reach Ethan's hands. Doing so with her ankles and hands bound was a challenge. She thought she might have made better progress if she could have lain on her belly and slithered like a snake. But the hold didn't allow for that much room with two other people present. So she made her way as best she could, planting her bound hands, moving one knee a few centimeters then the other knee to meet it.

"What are you doing?" Ethan murmured.

"Exercising so I don't get numb," she answered for the benefit of any potential listeners.

He snorted.

A good man. He could see the humor in little things even under dire circumstances.

Once she reached Ethan's back, she realized she couldn't get the right angle without pushing him onto his face. He protested.

"Sorry," she mumbled. "I couldn't help it."

She began to work at his wrists. His abrasions were new, his wrists and hands slick with fresh blood. Mel bit her lip against a wave of nausea. Usually, she didn't mind gore. Except this was someone she knew and liked. Someone she felt as though she had failed.

And they were such nice hands and wrists, broad and strong, the bones heavy, the muscles firm. Good hands for holding one up. Good hands for simply holding.

Stop, she silently admonished herself.

She got to work on his zip ties. He had pulled at them so much, they had stretched a little, though not enough to be useful. In fact, the stretch only created more problems. The clip was firmly embedded, the hole it had been slipped through elongated and narrowed, a different shape from the clip. The technique she'd used with Sheila wouldn't work.

And the van was slowing. A tollbooth or a turn into someplace remote, someplace where no one would hear gunshots?

The turn. Gravel crunching beneath the wheels. Likely a driveway. She might have mere seconds to free Ethan, let alone herself.

She grasped the plastic tie again. She needed to lift the loose end at the same time as she twisted the clip, then push. Lift, twist, push.

The tie slid free. She held on and added it to her waistband with the other one.

Ethan groaned and rolled onto his back. "My hands are numb, and my shoulders feel dislocated."

"Locate and wake them up fast," Mel murmured. "I think we're about to arrive somewhere."

As she spoke those words, the van slid to a stop with a spray of gravel.

"Quick," Ethan said, "put the zip ties on again."

Clever of her to figure out how to take them off, but their captors would have a better way to tie them up if they discovered them missing.

Sighing, she returned the strap to his wrists, looser this time. He might be able to work himself out of these on his own this time. She turned to Sheila, who was apparently still unconscious. Her progress toward his sister was slow, painstaking. Too slow. Footfalls crunched alongside the van. Someone was coming to open the hatch.

Mel murmured something indicating she had reached Sheila, then let out a whimper. "It's gone. The other tie is gone. I put it—"

The outside lock clicked open.

Ethan lay prone, unable to help her search the floor of the van for the other tie. He stayed motionless, listening to the thumps and scrabbling sounds of Mel's frantic search.

The latch popped.

"Got it," Mel whispered.

The hatch lifted. Light flooded into the van, artificial brightness from an outside security lamp. Even with his back to the direct glow, Ethan had to shut his eyes for a moment before he could bear the blinding glare. When he opened them again, he saw something small and shiny, and realized it was the brads on his shoes. Suddenly he wanted nothing more than to have those on his feet. If he got a chance to run again, he doubted he'd get far barefoot.

The *if* was so huge at this point, he figured bare feet were the least of his concerns. Sheila still hadn't moved or spoken. Mel was breathing hard, like someone who'd just run a four-minute mile. And he couldn't do much with his arms once again behind him, leaving them numb.

"Get them into the house," someone yelled from a short distance outside the van. The voice sounded like Derek's.

That realization didn't fill Ethan with confidence. They'd escaped from him once before. He'd ensure they didn't do it again.

"I'll take this one," one of the men from earlier said.

"Wimp." The other man almost sounded lighthearted, teasing. "She can't weigh more than a child."

Sheila then. She had been doing so much better before this, but she was still too thin. Ethan prayed this disaster didn't give her a setback.

"The big guy can walk," the first man said. "You get the other one."

A moment later, someone dragged him out of the vehicle until his feet hit the gravel. He was going soft. As a boy, he could walk over gravel without noticing it wasn't soft sand. As a man who wore boots or shoes all day, he felt every stone dig into his soles.

He definitely needed those shoes.

The walk to the house wasn't far. They marched along a dozen yards of gravel drive bathed in illumination, then up three steps to a porch. A wooden porch. Ethan added splinters to the stone bruises on his feet.

The structure appeared to be an old farmhouse, with a wooden screen door and painted storm door. A narrow entryway beyond that smelled of mildew. Whoever owned this house, they hadn't used it or cleaned it in a while. Dim electric lightbulbs overhead showed cobwebs in the corners and layers of dust on the floor.

Ethan took in every detail he could, from wallpaper—faded but still showing some kind of scrolling gold pattern—to the truly beautiful woodwork beneath layers of grime. No one seemed to mind him or Mel seeing the house or the men's faces.

Because neither of them—*none* of them, including Sheila—was expected to leave there alive.

"Keep going." The man behind Ethan prodded him in the spine with either a fist or a gun muzzle. Ethan couldn't tell. He kept moving, following the others—the men carrying Sheila and Mel.

The latter lifted her head from across her captor's shoulder and met his eyes. Hers were dark and red-rimmed, as though she'd been crying. Except he hadn't heard a sob from her or seen any evidence of tears. He had yet to see her cry despite what they had already endured. She was strong. Perhaps too strong. Her half smile told him to remain strong too.

She had figured out how to get off the zip ties once. She could do it again. His might be loose enough now to take off himself. He would try the minute they were all alone.

He hoped they would all be alone together. They needed to figure out how to get out of this fix. They would die if they didn't.

The men marched them up a flight of steps that creaked and groaned. The zip ties didn't allow Ethan to climb—there wasn't enough space between his feet to have them on different stairs. With a gun pointed at him, he climbed the stairs like a toddler—sitting on his backside and shifting his weight up one at a time. The guards snickered at him, but Ethan tried not to let it phase him.

At the top of the stairs and down a narrow hallway, they entered a room devoid of furniture. A single lightbulb hung from the ceiling, and the only window was too small for anyone but a child to pass through.

This wasn't a second floor; it was an attic. The roof space had been partitioned off somewhere along the years, but this room still held all the features of an attic, with a sloping ceiling, poor lighting, and that tiny window.

This wasn't the sort of place where anyone could keep a prisoner for long. The lack of even the barest of amenities drove that point home.

The door closed behind Ethan. A lock clicked into place. Sheila lay on the floor. Mel sat propped against a wall, eyes closed, and Ethan remained standing, afraid if he sat, he would never get up.

"Let me free you," Mel said. "You'll fall over if you stand there for much longer."

Ethan crossed the room. "I might be able to wiggle out. I think they're pretty loose."

"Not loose enough." She tugged and twisted. The plastic cut into his wrists, but then he was free, rubbing feeling back to his arms, flexing his shoulders.

Then he dropped to his knees beside his sister. "Sheila, can you hear me?"

"Loud and clear."

"You're okay." He wrapped his arms around her. "Thank You, Lord. Were you pretending to be out?" he asked.

"Most of the time. I wasn't sure it was you with us, and—" She lifted her head and stared toward Mel. "Who's she?"

"Mel Carter. She's a PI."

"A what?" Sheila's sweet, breathy voice filled the room too much.

"Shh," Ethan cautioned. "She helped me figure out where you were." He smiled at Mel. "And helped me out of a few jams along the way."

"Can she help us out of this one?" Sheila asked.

"Not with my hands and feet tied," Mel muttered.

"I'm sorry." Ethan set Sheila on the floor and turned to Mel. "How do you do this?"

With his own hands free and functioning, he was able to follow her instructions on the lift and twist effect, and freed her hands and feet. She began to rub both, so he turned to Sheila, freeing her as well.

"Are the boys all right?" Sheila asked. "Derek said… He said…" Her big green eyes filled with tears.

"They were fine last time I checked." Ethan worked off Sheila's hand restraints, and Mel removed the one around her feet. "But he's mentioned more than once that he'll go after them to make you talk."

Sheila looked at him, her eyes huge and liquid in the eerie light. "I can't tell him where the money is."

"Why not?" Mel's tone was a little sharp.

Ethan couldn't blame her.

"Because…" Sheila wiped her face on the sleeve of her shirt. "Because I don't know where it is."

ELEVEN

Mel stared at Sheila, mouth agape. She couldn't think past the echo of Sheila's claim she didn't know where the drug money was located.

Across from her, Ethan appeared just as dumbstruck. Dumbstruck and maybe a little angry. Spots of color glowed on his chiseled cheekbones and a white line formed around his mouth. Eyes closed, he tilted back his head. Mel suspected he was praying for patience or self-control.

"But Derek said—" He breathed hard through his nose. "He said you'd hidden it away. Why does he think that?"

"He knew the money was gone—he knew that I was the only one who could have gotten it, so I let him believe I still had it. He told me he would kill me for turning him in, but I figured if he thought I knew where the money was, he would keep me alive until I told him where to find it."

"But you could never tell him." Mel found her voice, though it sounded a bit squeaky in her ears. "You know he'd…hurt you if you did." She couldn't bring herself to use the word *kill*, not in regard to this fragile, sad woman, who was probably five years older than Mel but looked at least five years younger. "Hurt you and your family."

Sheila nodded without lifting her head.

"Then what did you do with the money?" Ethan asked.

"I turned it over to the cops, of course." She gave her brother a duh look.

"But it never came out in Derek's trial." Sitting cross-legged, Ethan drummed his fingers on his knees, his gaze fixed somewhere over his sister's head. "They mentioned they had recovered a few hundred dollars—nothing close to half a million."

"Then the cops stole it," Sheila said.

Mel wanted to protest, to defend the CPD. Her parents had worked for the Chicago PD. They had given their lives in the line of duty. They and their friends in the department would never do something like steal money.

Yet not all cops were honest. When evidence was collected from a crime scene, not all of it made it to the evidence locker.

Mel sighed. "It could have happened, and someone covered it up."

"After all these years," Ethan said, "no one will ever recover it."

"That's why we need to get away," Sheila wailed.

"Shh." Ethan smoothed tangled brown hair back from her face. "We all have to get away."

"And we need to be quiet about what we're planning," Mel whispered.

Sheila whimpered. "I'm cold."

So was Mel. The day had been warm, but the night,

especially out in the country, still held an early spring chill. None of them was dressed for temperatures in the forties. Ethan didn't even have his shoes.

Mel stood, attempting to work feeling into her feet, rocking from heel to toe, trying not to make too much noise. Her movements made the floor squeak.

Interesting. It only squeaked where she was standing. The rest of the floor hadn't when Sheila and Ethan walked across it.

Mel began to pace the chamber, using the light from that single bulb for a guide. Back and forth. Back and forth. Yes, only that one patch squeaked when she stepped on it.

"Avoid this area," she said. "The floor is weak. I don't want one of us breaking a leg falling through it."

"What does a broken leg matter?" Sheila sniffled. "They're going to kill us."

Probably, especially if they had heard Sheila admit she didn't know where the money was after all.

"I tried telling Derek I don't actually have the money." Sheila spoke up as though she'd read Mel's mind. "But he doesn't believe me. And now he's going to get the boys and use them to force me to talk. Only, I can't tell him what he wants to hear." She began to sob.

Ethan crossed the room to comfort her.

Mel stalked to the window. She could see through it if she stood on tiptoe. Not that there was much to see. Two vehicles sat in the drive, the van they had been carried in and some kind of sports car, sleek and low and gleaming. That would make a good getaway car, except it could only hold two people.

Beyond the halo of light, the world appeared pitch-black. Stars, if any were visible and not under cloud cover, couldn't compete with the brilliance of the lamps. Inside, the house seemed silent, but probably wasn't. From outside, Mel caught the distant howl of a coyote. Another canine answered, then a third, and then the three joined in a chorus.

Mel shuddered. She knew coyotes usually left people alone. Yet that howl was so haunting, it chilled her to the marrow.

So she, Ethan, and Sheila had to escape into that darkness—escape into the land of coyotes and who knew what other creatures. Out here in the middle of nowhere, they could easily come across snakes and bobcats and maybe a brown bear.

Shivering, she made herself focus on the window itself. It was maybe eighteen inches across but only about six inches high. Sheila might fit through. Mel might fit through. Ethan could never fit. And what awaited them on the other side? A straight and dangerous drop to the ground?

Mel felt along the sill, seeking a latch or other means to open the casement. Her fingers encountered a smooth frame. She slid her fingers up the sides as far as she could reach. Not far enough to find a release.

Maybe this window didn't open. The owner of the house might have sealed it.

Behind Mel, the room had grown quiet save for an occasional sniffle from Sheila. Mel started to turn toward the others but sensed rather than heard a presence close and knew it was Ethan.

"What did you find here?" he asked in a murmur.

"Nothing good. I don't think the window opens."

"Do you mind if I try?" Ethan touched her shoulder.

Mel jumped as though shocked by electricity and stepped aside. "Not at all."

Ethan examined the window as Mel had, running his hands along the frame. He could reach higher than she could, to the top of the narrow portal and along the highest side.

"No good," he agreed. "Besides, it's straight to the ground. Fifteen feet or so. I don't think any of us could jump that far without at least spraining an ankle."

"My thoughts exactly." Mel covered her face with her hands, wishing for the first time since her father's death that she could wail and howl like the coyotes. She didn't. She had shed all her tears with the deaths of her parents and the end of her engagement.

"We'll figure something out, Mel." Ethan's voice was so soft, he may as well have stroked her hair as he had Sheila's when he was comforting her. Then he did caress her hair, a featherlight smoothing from her temple to her ear. For the first time in her life, she wished for long hair so he had more to caress, so his touch would have a reason to linger.

When he dropped his hand to his side again, she felt bereft, isolated, alone.

"When do you think they'll come to us?" she asked.

"Early morning, most likely."

"So we need to get out of here tonight."

"Come on, let's go sit and ruminate on this." Ethan took hold of Mel's hand and led her across the room to where Sheila sat against the wall, her knees drawn up.

Just before Mel reached the wall, she stepped on the squeaky board in the room—and realized that the others right around it were squeaky too. Something must have weakened the wood in this spot. This...rather large spot, where the flooring seemed vulnerable.

"Ethan?" Mel got his attention then stepped on the squeaking board and the ones all around.

Ethan left Sheila and crossed the room. He crouched next to the particular floorboard and ran his hand along the edge, then began to pat his pockets. Something jingled. Change.

"They took my keys," he said, "but they left my wallet and change."

He drew a coin from his pocket and ran it around the edge of the board. Sheila crossed to crouch beside her brother. Her eyes gleamed in the light from the window.

Mel patted her own pockets. Wallet. No keys. They had taken anything that could be used as a weapon. The wallet would serve as identification when their bodies turned up tomorrow or in three days, three months...

She focused on what Ethan was doing, running the coin back and forth, back and forth, along the seam of the floorboard.

"What are you doing?" Sheila whispered.

"It's loose," Ethan murmured. He slipped the coin into his pocket. Gently, slowly, he rocked the piece of wood. It was loose indeed. It creaked then.

The house was oddly silent, as though they were the only ones there. Surely guards remained, but maybe they were sleeping or relaxing somewhere else in the house.

Counting on that, Ethan lifted the board again. A gust of dusty, dank air wafted up. The three of them peered into the hole. No light illuminated the space below. One of them had to reach in and risk feeling around.

"There could be live wires in there," Mel said.

"Not likely. If there are wires, they'll be shielded." Ethan stretched out on the floor facedown and extended his long arm into the hollow. The faintest scraping sound suggested he'd hit something below. "Acoustic ceiling tiles," he reported.

A ceiling into what?

"I can move one of them aside," Ethan said.

"There could be someone in the room below us," Mel cautioned. "Everyone be quiet."

Sheila and Mel stretched out opposite Ethan and peered into the darkness. Slowly, inch by inch, he slid the tile to one side. It scraped with each movement. With each scrape, Mel caught her breath and waited for a shout, even a shot. But nothing happened.

Light glowed from below, probably through a window, as with this room. The window below must be larger, as Mel spotted dark shadows of furniture—a chest, a bed, a desk. Someone's bedroom either now or in the past. No one appeared to be in the room at the moment.

"We…we'll have to pry up a few more boards to make the opening big enough, but I think I can manage that pretty easily now that the first one is out of the way," Ethan said. "And then…"

Ethan and Mel raised their heads at the same time. Their eyes met from a mere six inches apart. He released his breath and the warm air brushed her lips. Then they both smiled.

"Escape," Mel said.

* * *

Ethan decided to go first without asking either of the women. He was the tallest, so could lower himself to the floor more easily without landing with the thud the shorter women would make dropping a yard or so. He was also fairly good at hand-to-hand combat, if necessary.

Even with several boards removed, the opening was a tight fit for his shoulders, but he hunched forward and managed to squeeze through. The floor was a mere foot or so below his feet when he dangled through the hole. An old house with low ceilings. His bare feet made no sound on the wooden floorboards. Once standing, he waited, listening. Faintly, as though from a far room, he heard the low murmur of voices, then— music? He crept to the door and laid his ear against the panel. Somewhere down the hall, the guards were watching television. Good. The sound of the music and laugh track would help cover up any noise he and the others made.

He checked and, yes, the door locked from the inside. It was one of those old-fashioned locks that required a skeleton key to open. It wouldn't stop anyone from barging in for long but maybe just long enough.

Door secured as best he could without the racket of moving the chest in front of it, he crossed the room to the window and looked out. He wasn't sure how far from the ground the house would be on this side of the first floor. If the window was too high, they couldn't exit from it.

He slid up the sash. No screen. Just cold, fresh air smelling of new grass rushed into the room. The drop to the ground was far, but not terrible. Eight feet at the most, he estimated. But the light was bright, and the ground barren of shrubs or trees. They had no cover between the window and the automobiles. Not that they could drive the cars. They had no keys. They could only head to the darkness of the surrounding land, an unfamiliar terrain where the coyotes howled.

Ethan lowered the window, turned and struck his bare toes on something solid. Pressing his lips together over the impulse to exclaim at the pain, he looked down to see a suitcase lying on the floor, sideways, as though ready to be unpacked.

This room was being used by someone—someone who could return at any moment. They needed to move fast.

He headed back to the hole in the ceiling but paused long enough to inspect the top of the chest for anything useful. A weapon would be nice, but no guard worth even a grain of salt would leave his weapon behind.

He searched the dresser top. A wallet—Ethan wouldn't touch that. Other detritus from a man's pocket. A pack of gum, a disposable lighter…

And a single key.

Ethan didn't know what it was for. Maybe the van. Maybe the sports car. Either would do. They could drive it to the city, fetch his truck, head for Kentucky and his nephews…

He pocketed the key and the lighter. One never knew when one would need to start a fire.

Finally, he returned to the hole in the ceiling. "Come down," he whispered. "I'll catch you."

Moments later, Sheila's shiny ballet flats appeared. Ethan caught her by the waist, noting that she seemed even thinner than the last time he'd seen her a mere three days ago, and eased her to the floor.

"Go stand by the window," he murmured.

She nodded and moved away.

Ethan focused on the ceiling again. "Mel?"

"Coming, but I'm fixing the floor and the ceiling on the way down."

Of course she'd thought of that. Why immediately give away the means by which they'd escaped?

Her sneakers appeared, then jeans and fleece jacket. He caught her waist, clutching her in place while she moved the floorboards and ceiling tile back to their original positions. Holding her close like that, it was a struggle to keep from thinking about what a beautiful woman she was, and how fond of her he already was.

Fond? What a weak word for how Melissa Carter made him feel. And yet he had no room for romance in his life. Not when his family needed all of his attention. It wouldn't be fair to ask a woman to put up with his family always coming first.

A gentle clunk announced the lowering of the wooden attic floorboard, then the acoustic ceiling tile was carefully scraped into place. Ethan set Mel on the floor, and they stood together, listening for sounds of someone approaching the room.

Nothing other than the TV.

"Should we go?" Ethan asked.

Mel looked up at him, her eyes huge and dark in the ambient light. "I see no point in staying here." She gave him a faint smile, and he realized he still held her waist.

He dropped his hands to his side as though burned. "I—I'm sorry." He felt like a stammering schoolboy.

"No problem." She touched his cheek, her fingers

rasping on his day-old stubble. Then she was away, standing beside Sheila at the window.

Ethan joined them. "I can lower you two down. It's not far to the ground, but once you're outside, you'll have no cover. Run as fast as you can and hide behind the van."

"How will we get away?" Sheila asked.

"One step at a time," Ethan said, to cover for the fact that he didn't really have an answer for that yet. "Getting out of here is what's important now."

"Getting out of here without anyone seeing us," Mel said. "Stay below the window line."

"Run bent over?" Sheila asked. "Is that possible?"

"It is," Mel said. "I'll go first so you can watch."

She raised the window and swung a leg over the sill. Ethan gripped her forearms, and she slid off the sill to the ground. He leaned forward as far as he could so her drop was negligible. As soon as her sneakers hit dirt, she bent at the waist and raced on tiptoes toward the van. Her path took her past a large front window, most likely the room where the guards watched TV. Once she disappeared behind the bulk of the cargo van, Ethan waited with Sheila to see if anyone had noticed her. No one shouted out or raced to the front door. The television sounds continued.

"Ready?" Ethan asked Sheila.

She nodded.

She didn't start running the instant she touched the ground. She glanced from Ethan to the van, and back again, her face a mask of apprehension.

"Go," Ethan whisper-shouted.

She nodded then took off. Her hair flew behind her like a banner. Her leather-soled shoes crunched the gravel like a series of firecrackers. No way the guards wouldn't hear her. Ethan gave himself a mental smack. He should have told her to take them off. He should have—

Too late now. Someone had opened the front door, calling, "Who's out there?"

Nothing but the faint howl of a coyote.

The man looked left, toward the van. Mel and Sheila must be well hidden, for the man didn't move in that direction. Just in time, Ethan realized he would see the open window if he glanced right, so he closed it…and waited. Waited…

Then the front door closed with a bang. Someone shouted from within the house.

At that, Ethan threw open the window and escaped out of it as fast as possible, pausing only long enough to close it behind him. Then he was running, bent double, racing for the van. *Let the key work. Let the key work* was his prayer, repeated with the rhythm of his footfalls. Best case scenario, it would work for the van. The sports car would be faster, but it was also smaller. Too small for the three of them.

He reached the far side of the van just as the front door opened again. This time, footfalls echoed on the wooden boards of the porch. One of the guards had come outside to see what had caused the noises.

TWELVE

Mel peeked over the hood of the van. Someone had come out, was looking their way. They couldn't run fast enough to escape. Nowhere in the surrounding countryside could they find a safe place to hide.

Yet Ethan had a key fob. He flashed it in front of her face then clicked the button. The van chirped and its lights flashed. It was a huge signal to the bad guys what they were doing, but that didn't matter anymore. They already knew their prisoners had escaped the house.

"In!" Mel shouted.

Secrecy was no issue now.

She threw herself into the front seat of the vehicle and held out her hand. "Key."

"But—" Ethan began.

"Don't argue. I know this area better than you. It'll be easier for me to figure out where we are."

He dropped the key into Mel's hand. She slid across to the driver's seat and fired up the engine. Ethan and Sheila leaped in beside her. Before he had the door closed, Mel had released the parking brake and hit the gas.

That was when the first gunshot rang out. *Let them try.* Hitting a moving target wasn't easy, especially at night. And Mel was moving. She didn't bother with the driveway. She spun the wheel to the right and headed across the yard.

The vehicle bounced and jostled. Sheila slid between the seats with a grunt. Ethan nearly landed on his head in his effort to drag his door shut, then Mel accelerated and the door swung into place with a bang.

"Seat belts," Mel called. "This is going to be a wild ride."

Over the roar of the van's engine, she caught the sound of other gunshots. All went wild. No one had expected her to drive cross-country. But they hadn't had rain in a while and the ground was dry, hard. Lumpy with tufts of dirt and weeds, but easily drivable without worrying about being mired in mud as she moved in a wide swoosh toward the road.

The road. Which direction?

"Did we turn right or left into the driveway?" she asked.

"Right." Ethan sounded confident in that.

"They're going to catch us," Sheila whispered from the back seat, sounding panicked.

"Not if I can help it." Mel wished she dared drive without the headlights. In the darkness of the country, headlights were a beacon, a target, a call to say *Here we are. Shoot us.*

They had moved out of pistol range. She didn't know if they were far enough away that she couldn't hear the shots or if the men had given up on shooting at them. She couldn't think about what lay behind. She must think about what lay ahead. The road. Freedom, if they could make it.

The night was black beyond the halogen lights near the house. Mel had never seen such blackness. No moon or stars lent their light either. Must be cloud cover. Dense cloud cover. Only instinct led her to the road. And she hoped that instinct was right. She hoped she had a good sense of direction even from her introduction to the area from inside the window-less cargo bay.

The front tires bumped through a channel deep enough to be a ditch. On the other side, they spun on gravel. The driveway. They had made an arc back to the driveway. Mel gunned the engine harder. The back tires followed, fishtailing the van. She slowed enough to take control and turn the vehicle to the left, then hit the gas. In no more than a heartbeat, the terrain changed again, grew smooth and quieter beneath their wheels. Again, Mel swung the wheel to the left then began to speed up the road.

And from the side windows, all of them saw the sports car headed in the same direction.

"We can't outrun them," Sheila said, her voice low and tense. "I know that car. It's Derek's. It's super fast."

But not super safe. A patch of gravel, a slick of oil, and that car would go spinning off the road.

On the other hand, vans were notoriously top heavy.

Mel had never driven anything larger than an SUV, and this van was bigger. She didn't know how sturdy it was, how safe it was. She did know she had to keep it on the road and go as fast as she could manage without losing control. She doubted that was fast enough to outrun the sports car.

"We have to outsmart them," Ethan said as though reading her thoughts.

"They're gaining on us," Sheila announced.

Mel drove with one eye on the road ahead and one on her side-view mirror. The sports car was far too close. Not close enough for them to start shooting, but it would be soon. At least they were unlikely to be able to force the van off the road, with the van being so much larger and heavier a vehicle. But they could take out the van's tires if they were good enough shots.

None of them spoke. The silence inside the cab emphasized the roar of the engine. They were flying down the road. Seventy. Seventy-five. Eighty.

Still, the sports car drew nearer, yard by yard, car length by car length.

Mel eased the van to eighty-five. Eighty-six—

The vehicle began to shudder and shimmy as though shaking from cold.

"This is all the speed I can get out of her," Mel muttered.

She backed off a few miles per hour and tried again. This time, she managed eighty-seven. Not enough. That sports car could go at least a hundred and probably far more. The van's engine was too small for more power.

If she'd had her car, the sports car would be eating their dust, if they even got that close. But her car was gone, probably hauled off to some compound by now.

Mel shook off the regret and tried to peer left and right, seeking a place to pull off the road.

"If I turn off the lights and drive down a side road, I might fool them…or something," she thought aloud.

"You probably won't be able to stay on the road without headlights. Are you willing to take a bumpy ride?" Ethan flashed her a smile in the rearview mirror.

"I'm willing to do anything if it gets us away from them. That car's going to catch up with us in half a minute."

The distant headlights looked like the eyes of a monster glowing in the side mirror.

"I have an idea. It's a small chance," Ethan said. "It might not work at all, but it's worth trying."

"Okay, what?"

Ethan told her.

Mel tensed, fearing the consequences of what they were about to do. They could end up the ones in trouble.

"I'll tell you when." Ethan's voice was low and steady. "Be ready to make your move when I say so."

"I'm ready for anything."

The monster's eyes loomed closer, low and bright. Too bright. They had turned on their high beams, no doubt hoping to blind her with the reflection in her side mirror as they drew closer.

She kept her eyes ahead, concentrating on maintaining speed. She didn't know how Ethan would pick the right place. She couldn't see a thing outside their headlights' glow. The man must have eyes like a cat.

"Ready?" Ethan asked.

Mel's hands tensed on the steering wheel.

"Ease up your speed," Ethan continued.

Easing up went against all Mel's instincts with at least one armed man behind them and drawing closer, but she'd try anything.

"Let him get closer," Ethan said. "Or them. I doubt he's alone. They seem to travel in pairs."

Mel nodded and waited, reducing her speed a little more.

"Okay," Ethan said, voice still modulated low and calm. "Now."

Mel switched off the headlights and then spun the wheel to the right. Not too hard. She didn't want to roll the van. She made a smooth arc off the road, toward someone's property and a dip in the ground followed by a hedge.

She could no longer see the sports car out her side mirror.

"They're close enough," Ethan said.

Mel caught the flash of lights in the other mirror.

"Go." Ethan never raised his voice, never acted as though this was potentially a life-and-death situation.

Mel hit the gas. The van jounced and bounced across the drainage channel. Branches crackled and snapped, scraping along the sides of the van until they reached the other side.

"Keep going," Ethan said. "It seems to be an open field."

Mel continued to drive, though she thought her teeth might rattle from her head. She drove as far as she dared without lights. Afraid she would encounter trees or a fence, she turned the van halfway back, closer to the road. With the road visible ahead of them, they could see the sports car, low to the ground and as small as a child's toy, roar toward the break in the hedge…and halt. It was stuck.

For now.

Ethan gave himself a few seconds to study the bogged-down sports car. He'd taken a great risk in what he'd had Mel do. The car's engine might have been powerful enough to get it through the slight ditch and the hedge, especially after the heavier van plowed a path. But maybe the van had disturbed the earth enough to make the car's passage more difficult. Either way, Ethan doubted it would stay stuck for long.

"Let's get going," Ethan said. He kept his tone modulated, not wanting to upset Sheila or startle Mel.

She was an excellent driver—but that didn't surprise him. Everything about her impressed him.

He returned his attention to where it should be—ensuring they got away while they could.

"Be prepared for trouble," he told Mel.

"I know." She kept her gaze ahead. "We'll be within firing range." It was risky to drive close to the sports car—but it was riskier to continue driving off-road. All it would take would be a root or hole in the wrong place, and the van would get stuck. They were safer back on the road.

"Lie on the seat," Ethan told his sister. "You'll be safer below window level."

With a little whimper, Sheila flattened herself along the back seat.

Jaw tight in the dashboard lights, Mel leaned over the steering wheel and hit the gas. The van shot forward, swaying and bouncing through the field. Even with his seat belt on, Ethan had to grip his door armrest to keep from flopping to the side or forward against the glove box. His teeth rattled and snapped together, nearly catching his tongue.

Then they reached a parallel position with the sports car. Two men stood beside it, looking down at the frame bottomed out on the ground. One glanced up at their passing and grabbed for his weapon. A flash, a bang, the ping of a bullet hitting the cargo bay.

Sheila gasped.

"We're okay," Ethan said, though he wondered where the gas tank was located. "We'll be okay."

"Speed up," Sheila commanded.

"I'm trying." Mel spoke through clenched teeth. Concentration. Stress.

Ethan feared she couldn't keep up this pace for much longer. She needed to go home, needed to rest.

Except she couldn't go home now. Derek's men knew who she was—and they would know where to look for her. He had dragged her into this mess, and she was stuck until they figured out how to end it.

Ethan knew how to stop Derek and his henchmen. It was dangerous. It was risky. It might not even work, and they could all end up dead, with his nephews in the hands of their felonious father.

But he had to try.

At last, the blacktop hummed beneath their front tires. The back ones spun on the edge of the drainage channel. From no more than fifty feet away, one of the men fired again.

"Ease off," Ethan directed. "Back up just a little…"

Despite the shots pinging off the cargo hold, Mel followed his directions. The shooter was aiming for the tires. He wasn't a good shot, apparently, since his aim was too high.

The seconds it took for the back tires to grip the road felt like an hour. Ethan found himself leaning forward as though doing so would help the van lift itself onto the pavement. A glance to his left showed him Mel was doing the same thing. For a heartbeat, he and Mel shot one another a smile of triumph, of understanding, of something warmer.

Sheila leaned over the console between Mel and Ethan. "Stop making googly eyes at each other and let's go. They're going to get out of there quick enough."

Mel nodded and hit the gas.

Ethan didn't bother to deny the googly eyes comment even though the look they'd exchanged hadn't been anything of the kind. Regardless, his face felt hot.

"Now what?" Sheila asked.

"If we have enough gas," Mel said, "we'll get far enough into the city to catch an L train. We can lose ourselves in the city."

Sheila persisted. "Lose ourselves to where?"

"I don't know," Mel admitted. "My boss. The cops."

"I don't trust the cops," Sheila said. "Derek had too many of them in his pocket. And the ones who weren't crooked…they were just indifferent. The night I got Derek arrested wasn't the first time I called 9-1-1. It was just the first time they'd actually come. The dispatcher heard the babies crying—that was what finally got them to act."

Ethan knew this story. Sheila had told him a hundred times. She'd felt lost, abandoned, uncared for. No matter how often he tried to reassure her, she believed she was fighting the world, fighting Derek, on her own.

"I have a better idea than staying in the city," Ethan said.

Mel glanced at him, and the van swerved. "Sorry." She corrected her steering. "Don't say it. 'Eyes on the road.'"

No one said it.

Ethan reached across to turn on the headlights.

"Wait." Mel raised one hand from the wheel to indicate the horizon. "Do you see lights ahead?"

"Is it sunrise?" Sheila asked.

"City glow," Ethan said, unable to keep the dislike from his voice. "It's unnatural."

"The darkness like out here scares me," Mel admitted. "I need lights around me."

"But with the city lights, you never see the stars," Sheila protested. "How could you live without seeing the stars?"

"I couldn't have said it better." Ethan reached back to pat Sheila's shoulder. "As for my plan…" He turned on the headlights just in time for them to see a railroad crossing ahead. The gate was down, and the distant wail of a train whistle echoed through the night.

Mel slammed on the brakes. "We don't need a delay like this. I could drive around the gate."

"No," Sheila and Ethan said together.

"We had a cousin do that and get stuck," Ethan explained. "He got out of the way in time, but his car was nothing but scrap metal."

"And we'll be nothing but buzzard food if those guys catch us." Mel began to drum a shuffle rhythm on the wheel. "I can't even see the train. They didn't need to put the gate down so soon."

She leaned over to study her side mirror.

Ethan did the same with his. If she saw the lights he did, she didn't say anything, possibly not to frighten Sheila.

Lights didn't mean their pursuers were closing in

on them. It could easily be another driver. But there was just no way to be sure.

And the train was still not in sight.

"Come on. Come on. Come on." Mel practically vibrated the van with her intensity. "See, I would have had time to go around."

Or maybe not. The train seemed to come out of nowhere in a breath, barreling across the highway at breakneck speed. Engine hulking. Car after car after car. They seemed to stretch to infinity. Another engine appeared in the line.

And two sets of headlights glowed in the side mirrors. One set was high, like an SUV or a pickup. The other was low—maybe the sports car.

And Ethan, Mel, and Sheila couldn't move in the van because the train and its dozens of cars and multiple engines was still rumbling past.

THIRTEEN

Mel watched the train, counting cars to stop herself from doing something useless like screaming in frustration and fear. Those men were close behind. They might do nothing with another vehicle in proximity, but they might not care. They had, after all, walked into a café and started shooting it up in broad daylight. Carjackings took place all the time. The driver of the SUV might never realize what had happened.

Five hundred. Six hundred. Her counting made no sense. She had no idea how many cars she had counted. The train seemed like it would go on forever, a never-ending string of cars and engines. Too many cars of the train ahead and too much of the sports car behind. What were they waiting for?

Mel curled her fingers around the steering wheel hard enough to hurt. She needed to be ready to take off as soon as the gate lifted.

Or maybe…

"Do you trust me?" she asked Ethan.

"Yeah, I do." His voice held a tone of surprise and certainty.

"Then hang on."

In the distance, she caught the lights of the caboose. Ten cars away. Nine. Eight… One… The caboose slid between the gates blocking the road.

And Mel hit the gas and swerved over into the on-coming lane where there was no traffic. They left the road, bouncing over a rough, a gravel shoulder, then the tracks. The train moved so slowly, the caboose was mere feet away.

She focused on the crossing. Over tracks. Two sets. Around the gate and back onto the road. Another vehicle coming in the opposite direction flashed its lights and blared its horn. Mel ignored it. It had to stop anyway. In seconds, she was back in the right lane and flying down the highway.

"Tell me what you see," she said.

"Trying to follow." Ethan sounded a little tense. "But that SUV is in the way, and now there's a car in the opposite lane blocking them from getting through."

Mel huffed out a sigh of relief. "Then it worked."

"It was a risky move," Ethan pointed out.

Mel laughed. "You think? It was all I could think of."

"I was about to suggest it."

"Did we get away?" Sheila asked.

"For now," Ethan said. "For now."

"We have a head start," Mel said, trying to be positive.

They had had a head start earlier, too, but that sports car had some muscle—enough to get it out of sticky spots. The van's engine was kind of wimpy. But she had learned to drive from the best—her father—and she pushed the van to the limit and then a little more. If a cop came out of nowhere and pulled them over, so much the better. They could tell their story and have some protection.

If they had a cell phone, they could call the police. But those had been confiscated. If they lost their pursuers in the city, Mel planned to stop somewhere and buy a disposable one. If they had any money and not just credit or bank cards that could be traced.

"Did they leave you any money?" Mel asked Ethan.

"I don't know." He pulled his wallet from his pocket and flipped it open. "So they're thieves right alongside being drug dealer henchmen."

"Took all your cash?" Mel felt a little sick.

"Yep. And my credit cards and bank card."

"Those are traceable anyway." Mel took one hand off the wheel long enough to pull her own billfold from her pocket and toss it to Ethan. "Will you check this?"

He checked, pausing for a moment before looking in the money department.

"Nothing," he said. "They left your transit card."

"Great."

But not having any cash was a problem. She needed to figure out how they could get some.

"I have some money." Sheila spoke up from the back seat.

Ethan shifted in his seat. Mel tried to watch through the rearview mirror, but she was beginning to see traffic ahead and needed to concentrate on the road and other vehicles.

"How so?" Ethan asked.

"I had cash on me to buy some groceries, remember? I didn't use it all."

"How much?" Mel asked.

"About fifty dollars," she answered.

Not much. Not enough to get them very far. They couldn't hole up in a cheap motel until they could persuade the police to help them. They couldn't get a cell phone and eat too.

Suddenly, Mel was starving. She couldn't remember the last time she'd eaten. Her lunch with Ethan had been interrupted before they'd even ordered. That felt like a lifetime ago. Her stomach cramped. Her head spun. Beneath her hands, she felt the steering wheel turn without her meaning to do so, and the van swerved.

"I've got to slow down," she murmured.

"You're tired," Ethan said.

"I'm hungry." Mel eased up on the gas. "We're in the suburbs now. They'll have a harder time catching up with us here."

"What are we going to do?" Sheila asked.

"Find an L station." Mel checked her side mirror. Several cars followed them. Despite the growing light from gas stations and strip malls, she couldn't work out if any of them were the sports car. She didn't think so. Or maybe that was wishful thinking.

"But it's the middle of the night," Sheila said. "How can we take a train?"

"The Red Line runs all night."

How could Sheila have lived in Chicago for years and not known that?

"I never took the train," Sheila said as though Mel had asked the question aloud. "They scare me."

Ethan laughed. "You drive like a NASCAR racer

through mountain roads, but you're scared of the L train?"

"I'm not in control," Sheila said. "I'd feel better if I was driving the train."

"Makes sense to me." Mel smiled.

The smile quickly faded. She didn't drive through the south suburbs much, hadn't been there in years. She didn't know her way around. She didn't have GPS.

"Ethan, will you look in the glove compartment and see if there's a city map?"

Ethan popped open the glove box. Objects cascaded across his legs and onto the floor. From the corner of her eye, Mel caught sight of a couple of Hershey's bars, a fat envelope, and a pistol. Ethan bent to retrieve it, and Mel grasped his arm, stopping him.

"Our fingerprints will be all over the van, but we don't want it on any of that stuff, especially the gun," she pointed out.

"What about the candy?" Sheila said, sounding eager.

Mel grinned. "Just try to stop me."

They gathered up the candy bars and tore open the wrappings, stuffing the paper into their pockets and the chocolate into their mouths. Mel steered them into a side street as they consumed the cheap fuel of chocolate and sugar as though it was fine dining.

Once they had eaten one apiece, crunching the almonds like a pack of hungry squirrels, Mel headed out on the main streets again in search of a business that was open and looked capable of providing directions to the nearest L station. A gas station seemed like their best option, but the teenager behind the counter of the first one had no idea where the L station was.

He didn't think it ran to the south side. Mel rolled her eyes and tried a bakery, a coffee shop, and a dry cleaner. No one could give them directions. For all she knew, they were headed too far east or west or even north.

"We're leaving too much of a trail," Ethan said after the fourth business.

"I know." Mel beat her fingers on the steering wheel. "I rely on my phone too much to memorize directions anymore."

"Let's try one more gas station," Ethan suggested. "I'll go in."

Mel compressed her lips, but she understood. Sometimes a man could get directions from another male easier than a woman could. She didn't have to like it; it was just fact.

Except, Ethan had no shoes.

He glared at his feet as though the absence was their fault. "I forgot. They should be in the back. I can go—"

"You can't walk on this oily asphalt," Sheila protested. "I'll get them. Is there a lock release up here?"

Mel found it on the dashboard and popped the hatch. Sheila slid out and headed for the back. Despite Ethan's protests, Mel headed to the front and the clerk. He was a little older and, to her relief, he knew his way around the area.

"About a mile away, ma'am," he said then proceeded to give her precise directions. "Need gas?" he concluded.

"I don't—" She started to admit she had no money, but she hadn't looked at the gas gauge. She didn't know when the van had been last filled or how much fuel it carried or consumed. They'd driven quite a long way and at a high speed.

Sheila had some money. Mel could get the smallest amount of gas possible, just to ensure they reached the L.

She ducked her head. "Just five dollars' worth. I have to go out to get the money from the—"

"Melissa." Sheila yanked open the gas station door, her eyes were wild, her face white. "They—they—" She pointed.

Mel followed her gesture and her blood ran cold.

At the intersection, waiting for the light to turn and allow them access to the gas station lot, was the sports car.

They were on the run again. Shoving his socks into his pockets—he didn't have time to deal with them when they needed to run—Ethan jammed his feet into his shoes, grabbed Sheila's hand on one side and Mel's on the other, and raced around the far side of the gas station. The pavement was buckled, a serious tripping hazard, but he didn't slow down. If one of them stumbled, he bodily held them upright and kept going.

"We were so close." Mel sounded heartbroken.

She was breathing hard. They were all breathing hard. Sheila wheezed like a fireplace bellows with a leak. She was flagging, dragging back on his hand.

"I...can't." She pressed her hand to her side and stopped, doubled over. "Pain."

"Sheila, honey, we can't stop." Ethan rested his hands on her narrow shoulders, wishing he could impart some of his own physical vitality into her delicate frame. "If they saw us…" He trailed off. Of course they had seen him and Sheila and Mel. Or at least, they would have seen the van. It was hard to miss.

"Can you carry her?" Mel asked.

Ethan wasn't sure he could carry his sister and run at the same time. He was exhausted. He hadn't had anything to eat, except that candy bar, in nearly twenty-four hours. Yet he saw no choice.

He stooped so she could reach his back. "Climb on."

She hesitated. "Just leave me behind. This is all my fault anyway. You and Melissa shouldn't have to suffer more because of me."

"No," Ethan said emphatically.

"You have two children who need their mom," Mel said.

"But if I hadn't lied to save my own skin…" Sheila began to cry.

"Come on, Shee," Ethan coaxed her. "Climb on. We're not leaving you here alone. Either you come with us, or we all wait here."

"It's only a mile to the L train." Mel tried to be positive. She looked nearly as fragile and drawn as Sheila.

The rumble of a powerful engine on the other side of the gas station had them all swiveling their heads to stare in that direction. It sounded like the sports car. They had to get away and fast.

"Maybe we'll spot a cop on the way," Mel said.

"Maybe." Wiping her eyes on her sleeve, Sheila grasped Ethan's shoulders and hauled herself onto his back.

He straightened and set off, Mel trotting along beside him. They weren't running. A light jog was all they could manage. He hoped it would be enough.

"Let's stay behind buildings as much as possible," Mel suggested. "It's darker, but it'll make us harder to spot or get to."

The terrain was also rougher. Mostly, the space was parking slots often separated by strips of grass, even shrubbery. The former, they could cross. The latter, they had to circumvent, sometimes leading them closer to the street, closer to the streetlights. This kept up for two blocks before Mel held up her hand to stop. "Each block in Chicago is approximately an eighth of a mile. That means we have around six blocks to go."

"I'm all right," Ethan said.

"I can go that far," Mel said. "But we have to turn here and cross a major intersection. We're going to be exposed." She looked up at him, and her eyes were dark and shadowed in the first gray light of morning. "They may suspect we're headed for the L. The gas station attendant might have even told them we asked for directions there."

"And another station is too far away?" Ethan asked.

"I don't know. Another half a mile at least."

"Could we get a taxi?" Sheila asked. "Just to get us to the next station? My money should stretch that far."

"We need that to eat," Mel said. "And we might be safer on foot. Easier to get in and out of places."

Ethan nodded. "I agree." He released his hold on Sheila with one hand and grasped Mel's shoulder. "You're a right good trooper, Mel."

She smiled up at him, a genuine, warm smile, and he suddenly felt as though he could climb the natural bridge in Kentucky.

They tried to stroll up to the corner as though they were out for nothing more than a morning coffee run. Halfway there, Sheila insisted on being let down. "We'll stand out less if I'm walking too," she pointed out, which made so much sense, he let her. If they had to run again, he could pick her up.

If? *When* they had to run again.

He felt as though he was going to forever have nightmares about running through city streets.

Focus, he warned himself.

They were reaching the intersection. No pedestrians might be out, but cars had emerged in droves—cars that rattled and smoked, cars that glided in near silence, SUVs that tried to dominate the lanes, and an occasional tractor trailer sending everyone scurrying out of its way. The noise was overwhelming. Ethan wondered if people who lived there had ever heard a bird greet the dawn or fallen asleep to a chorus of crickets in the summer.

The light changed and they headed across the traffic. He and Mel looked left and right, seeking either the van or the sports car. Ethan saw nothing. Mel shook her head, as though acknowledging she had seen nothing either.

They crossed both ways and headed up the next block, seeking a path into the backs of the buildings. The area was getting into more traditional city architecture, the old city, with barely a man's breadth between buildings and alleyways behind. Mel led them down the nearest alley. Hearing the screech and clang of a trash truck, Ethan tensed, remembering the last time they had tried to get around one of those. It hadn't ended so well for him.

Sheila clung to his hand. It reminded him of her

boys when he took them to the general store. His general store. His business he was so proud of building and would keep building. The twins loved to "help" him there. They were so trusting, so innocent.

Sheila was trusting him to get her out of this mess. He had been so sure that he would. Now, he had his doubts. If that sports car came racing up the alleyway, they wouldn't be able to get away fast enough. Three shots and they'd all be dead.

Ethan forced himself not to run. He needed to conserve his energy for the next time danger found them. It probably wouldn't take long.

"My truck should still be in your neighborhood," Ethan said.

"You mean by the office?" Mel asked.

"Yep. By the B and B where I was staying. I paid through last night, so it should still be there."

"But you don't have any keys," Sheila said.

"I have one magnetized to the undercarriage."

Mel snorted. "Then it may not be there. Everyone puts their keys in a magnetic case under the car."

They had reached the end of the block. Mel held up her hand for them to wait and crept around the edge of the building, peeking left and right. The street before them was quiet, lined with parked cars. Ethan checked, but none was the sports car lying in wait for them.

"I think it's clear," Mel said.

They crossed and kept going. One more block, two. Then they slipped down the gangway between two houses and headed toward the next alley. Ethan caught the rattle and high-pitched squeal he had heard before—an elevated train. Close. So close.

"Two blocks," Mel said.

Then, just one.

They reached the end of the final block and approached the curb. The entrance to the station was right across the way. Also right across the way, half blocking their passage to those turnstile gates into train access, sat the van that had brought them back into the city.

FOURTEEN

Mel's instinct was to turn and run. Except, where would they go? Behind them lay nothing useful. Ahead of them lay danger.

"They want me," Sheila said in a voice so small Mel barely heard it above the roar of the next train sweeping into the station. "I'll give myself up while you go ahead and get on the train."

"They want me too," Ethan said.

"I know." Sheila began twisting the ends of her already tangled hair. "To make me talk. But if I tell them I'm ready to talk… Well, maybe they'll let the two of you go."

"Not likely." Mel grasped each of their hands and drew them away from the corner and into the shadow of a building. "We have to distract them or elude them somehow."

"I'll run up to the van and tell them the money is someplace," Sheila suggested.

Don't you think you've told enough lies? Mel barely stopped the words from flying from her mouth. Snapping at Ethan's sister wouldn't do them any good.

"No one is going near that van," Ethan said. "Is

there another way to get into the station?" He turned
to Mel.

"Around the block, maybe. I've never been in this
one before. Besides, they could be there too—one
guy in the van, one in the sports car. Or maybe more
than one. They would have had time to call in rein-
forcements."

"Then we have to distract them." Ethan looked
thoughtful, and a gleam brightened his green eyes.
"I know you run pretty fast, Mel. You're tired, but
can you still?"

"What do you have in mind?" Mel asked.

He told her, concluding with, "It might not work,
but it's our best shot."

"I'm game." Mel smiled.

"I thought you would be." He smiled back, and she
felt a wave of warmth wash over her, buoying her up
for the task ahead. She didn't have time to explore her
unusual reaction at the moment. She had a role to play.

She removed her transit authority card from her
wallet and handed it to Ethan. "Run it through twice
for the two of you."

Ethan took the plastic card from her, and she
headed for the curb.

She didn't wait for the light. As soon as she hit
the curb, she started to run. Car horns blared at her,
brakes squealed. A tin can of a foreign economy car
barely missed running into her. Uncharitably, she
thought she would have done more damage to the
vehicle than it did to her if it had crashed into her.
Then she was abreast of the van, racing up its side
and around the back.

She didn't think that would stop them from seeing

her. It just might give her ten seconds or so. Every second counted.

She was right. They did see her. She cleared the rear bumper seconds before the driver's-side door popped open.

"Halt!" someone shouted.

As if she would.

She kept running toward the station. And she began to scream for help.

The scattering of people heading into the station turned and stared at her, faces startled, coffee cups poised. One woman dropped her cup. Chai pooled on the concrete floor, scenting the normally musty air with cardamom. Mel leaped over the puddle of milky liquid, entered one of the gates into the platform access, then vaulted the turnstile.

"Miss, stop! You can't do that." The customer service agent shot from her booth, waving her arms. "Stop!"

"I can't. I can't," Mel cried. "Those men have guns and they're chasing me."

"You still have to pay," the agent persisted. She stepped in front of Mel, blocking her passage to the steps, arms crossed. "I don't see no men after you."

"They're back there." Mel waved toward the van. "They tried to drag me into the van."

"They ain't supposed to be parked there." Brows drawn together, the agent glanced from Mel to the van and back to Mel.

One of the men was coming toward the station.

Mel waved at him. "Look. That's one of them. He's coming this way."

The agent grabbed for her radio, speaking into it with rapid-fire words and codes.

Meanwhile, a crowd had formed around the agent and Mel, men and women and a few teens heading to work and school. Above, the tracks began to vibrate with the approach of a train. Passengers glanced up, anxious to get on board and not be late in their morning commute.

Mel slipped back, blending into the crowd. Her lack of stature made this easy. Tucked behind three tall men dressed in business casual, she was no longer visible to the agent—or, hopefully, to the attacker. Enough people crowded behind, and she doubted anyone could see her from the street side of the gates either.

This was the flaw in the plan. Ethan and Sheila couldn't see her. They were unfamiliar with the system. They might go the wrong way to the platform.

Lots of flaws in the plan. The crowd might not be large enough to hide them from their pursuers... Security might show up faster than any of them anticipated...

Mel couldn't think of all the things that could go wrong. She needed to move, to proceed as though everything would go right.

She slid along the tiled wall, head down to make herself even shorter. Her hair might draw attention. She needed to carry a cap with her, something to cover her hair. Or wear a hoodie. But there was nothing she could do about that now.

She moved through the station, finding her way to the far flight of steps. Up she climbed, her legs suddenly feeling like lead pipes in the sun—soft and heavy. She could sleep right there and then, or grab a half-eaten bagel discarded on the platform and eat it. In all her work, she had never experienced such fatigue and hunger. Nor such fear. Every passenger clattering up the steps after her potentially spelled danger. One of the men pursuing them could have gotten through the gate and found her. Or security could have arrived to arrest her for creating a disturbance.

That wouldn't be so bad. They needed the help. She intended to run up to the first cop she saw and beg for protection.

She saw neither pursuers nor police. Nor did she see Ethan and Sheila. Sheila would be easy to miss. But Ethan, not so much. He was tall and burly, so he'd stand out in a crowd.

That was a problem if he wanted to blend in.

She paused at the top of the steps, trying to see to the floor below. No good. Her view was too limited, and others were climbing the steps behind her. Friend or foe or unfamiliar strangers?

She put her back to the metal structure separating the head of the steps from the platform and watched each person who passed. So many people. Not so many business types heading away from the city. Tired men and women coming from nighttime work, yawning and rubbing their eyes, appearing as though they would fall asleep the instant they sat in a car.

Across the station, a train pulled in, heading for the city. All Mel's senses strained in a wish to be on that one, moving away from danger, moving toward what was familiar to her. The trip into the Loop would be around thirty minutes or maybe longer. She could maybe catch a catnap—

A hand grasped her arm. She started, realizing she had nearly fallen asleep where she stood. She opened her eyes to see a stranger peering down at her from behind mirrored glasses.

Mirrored glasses when the sun was just now coming up?

She straightened, on alert now. "Please remove your hand from my arm."

"Oh, I don't think so." The grip increased. "You need to come with me."

One of the bad guys then. Not one she had met as of yet, but not one to trust.

"Are you security? Are you police? Are you FBI?" She flung the questions at him rapid-fire, like blows. "Because if you're not, take your hand off me or I'll scream. I'll scream or worse."

The man laughed. "You're adorable. Now turn around, and let's go quietly down the steps, and my friends won't shoot your friends."

"You wouldn't risk a shooting in a crowded train station." Mel hoped not, anyway. And she definitely hoped he was bluffing about having caught Ethan and Sheila.

She had to risk it.

Another train pulled into the station, one headed out of the city. The people still on the steps hurried toward the platform, streaming past Mel and the man gripping her arm. In one, two, three seconds, the steps would be empty, and she could make her move without hurting anyone else.

"For the last time," she said through clenched teeth, "let me go."

He didn't, and she screamed. The station was tile and concrete with high ceilings. Her cry echoed like a siren. The man reared back, and Mel punched him in the throat. Left-handed, not as effective as she hoped, but still effective enough to send him reeling backward and stumbling halfway down the steps. He caught himself on the rail, Mel noted from the corner of her eye, but she couldn't worry about that now. She was already running for the train, grabbing the closing door and swinging aboard as the last warning bells rang, the doors slammed, and the train picked up speed out of the station.

She had gotten out of the station, had gotten away, yet she had no idea where Ethan and Sheila were, which meant she had to take the risk of going back.

Ethan caught sight of Mel diving into the opposite train. He and Sheila huddled behind a newspaper machine, watching the steps, watching the far platform. They had eluded the men once. That didn't mean they were safe. Their pursuers might still be in the station. That Mel had jumped aboard a train at the last minute without him and his sister suggested she had seen something. Someone.

"What do we do now?" Sheila whispered.

Ethan didn't answer right away. He kept his gaze on the platform across two sets of tracks. If only they could cross that way instead of having to return downstairs and go around to climb up again.

"Ethe." Sheila tugged on his sleeve.

"We get on the next train," he decided aloud.

"But the men—"

Were on the opposite platform. Ethan watched them. Three men—two familiar, the other a stranger in mirrored glasses who kept rubbing his neck. They conferred at the top of the steps, then spread out along the platform as though intending to enter different cars on the next arriving train. They were facing Ethan and Sheila now. Ethan stepped behind a pillar to watch them. He would know the instant one of them spotted him or Sheila.

"We have to get on the next train," he told his sister.

"But what about Melissa? Where do we go?"

"We'll figure it out."

The platform began to quake beneath their feet, signaling the train's approach. With or without Mel, they had to get on it. Those men were bound to see him and Sheila eventually. The station was filling up again, the crowd serving as a comforting shield. They could slip aboard unnoticed...

The train stopped with the space between two cars in front of them. One of the men caught sight of Ethan in the gap. Their eyes locked for a fraction of a second, then the man was racing for the steps, and Ethan was racing for the car door, his hand gripping Sheila's, nearly dragging her behind him.

They found sideways seats and dropped into them. Ethan's legs wobbled with fatigue. He suspected Sheila was tapping into her last reserves as well. Through the opposite windows, he watched the other two men speed toward the steps. They shouldn't have enough time to go down and back up again. They couldn't possibly have enough time. If Ethan and Sheila stuck to the same train, they would be ahead of them. Mel had told him this one would take them all the way to where her office was located. His truck was just a few short blocks from there. He and Sheila could take off for Kentucky.

Without Mel.

The idea left him feeling hollow. If they left, would he ever see her again? But maybe that would be the best thing for her. Going with them spelled danger for her. She didn't deserve what she had gone through. Not that he or Sheila did, either, but Sheila was family. Ethan endured what he must for her. He couldn't pay Mel enough for what she had already suffered because she'd agreed to help him. Leaving her behind worked the best for all concerned. He would only have one person to worry about on the trip southeast. A pity the idea made him so unhappy.

Sheila fell asleep, slumping against him. Ethan remained upright, watching, always watching—fellow passengers, the station platforms they entered, the doors on the sides of the train, and the emergency exits on the ends. Men walked through from one car to the next, begging for change. Few people gave them anything. They all looked like they needed a hot meal and so much more.

At the second station they passed through, Ethan caught sight of a policeman lounging on the platform as though he had nothing better to do. Ethan vaguely considered getting off the car and asking him for help. By the time he made up his mind, the brief stop ended and they were picking up speed for their next stop.

Still studying the retreating figure of the cop, Ethan missed the opening of the door at the end of the car until he sensed movement and jerked his head around to inspect the newcomer.

It was Mel. She strutted into the car, head down, hands in jeans' pockets, eyes darting right and left. When she spotted him, she straightened and smiled, and the sun blazed through the eastern windows as though her smile had raised it high enough to shine over the roofs of the buildings.

"I had to backtrack on an express train, but I thought I'd catch up with you eventually." Mel held out her hands.

Ethan took them and rose from his seat. In the middle of the car, they stood grinning at one another as though they didn't need to worry about gunmen tracking them down and tying them up again, or worse.

At that moment, for precious seconds, Ethan didn't care. Mel was with him again.

Then the train jerked to a halt in the middle of the track, throwing them off balance. They laughed and dropped onto the seats.

The movement woke Sheila, and she stared at Mel. "How?" she asked.

"I got on one train and looked for you. You weren't on it, so I waited for the next one, and here you are." Mel yawned. "I had a run-in in the station."

"So did we," Sheila said. "They saw us."

"They were on the other side, though," Ethan added. "I expect they're right behind us on the next train."

"We can change trains downtown," Mel said. "That should throw them off long enough for us to get to your truck."

"What then?" Sheila asked.

"We'll head for Kentucky and stop somewhere for rest and food," Ethan said. He turned to Mel. "You can stay here."

Mel stared at the passing city then faced Ethan. "I don't think I can. I've seen them—I can identify them. They have every reason to want to get rid of me too."

That left them all silent for several minutes, then she glanced at the station board and said, "We're going underground in a few minutes. Just thought I'd warn you."

She barely finished what she was saying when the train plunged into a tunnel. The rumble of wheels on track grew louder, echoing against the tiled walls. The lights were bright against the outside darkness of the tunnel, making Ethan feel exposed, trapped.

"How long?" he asked.

"A while, but we'll get off in a couple more stops and change trains."

They sat in silence, watching the stations pass, watching the people pass. At last, Mel stood, signaling they should get off. They followed her from the car and up an escalator. Back through the turnstiles.

"Still have my card?" Mel asked.

Ethan pulled it from his pocket.

Mel took it and ran it across the reader. "To pay for the trip for me. They'll never know, but my conscience is clear."

A screech of brakes below drew their attention. Another train was pulling in right behind theirs.

Mel sighed. "Let's go. They could be on that one."

"Do we never get a break?" Sheila said with a sigh.

Ethan and Mel didn't answer. He suspected she was thinking the same thing—they could use one, but one didn't seem to be likely. At least, not any time soon.

Mel led them up two flights of steps, down a short bit of sidewalk in the blessedly clear, cool air, and past buses and throngs of people, then up more steps to a platform high above the city. Sheila stumbled twice on the last flight, and barely picked up her feet as they passed through the gate onto yet another platform.

"How do you live like this?" Ethan asked.

Mel shrugged. "It's just the life I know. I like it. I like people and moving fast."

"I like moving fast too." Sheila yawned. "Especially if the road curves."

"She drives like she's operating every car as a roller coaster." Ethan made himself smile. "We have lots of curves in the mountains."

Mel shuddered. "I'd be terrified."

"I have been a few times, but she's an amazingly safe driver for all her speed."

"I'd never hurt anyone," Sheila said. "I didn't mean to hurt y'all."

"We know." Mel squeezed her hand.

She was such a kind woman to be so patient with his sister when he was sure she must want to wring Sheila's neck. Or at least give her a few strong words. Mel must understand that Sheila needed kindness more than anything.

Trains began pulling into the station. Orange. Green. They ignored those. Then Mel pulled them aboard one that said Purple.

No one had followed them so far. They could relax for the moment. Twenty minutes on the train, no more, Mel assured them. The view was good; a park with trees coming into their leaves, and always the lake in the distance. Ethan could almost breathe normally. Then they were off the train and on pavement in a neighborhood Ethan recognized. Four blocks to where his truck was parked.

"Let's take a bus," Mel said. "The less we're visible, the better."

They caught a bus in front of the station and rode the few blocks to where his truck was parked.

Where his truck *had* been parked.

Instead of the hulk of his battered, extended-cab pickup, the parking space he'd been assigned upon checking into the B and B was empty.

FIFTEEN

Mel fought the urge to slump her shoulders so far that she would end up sitting on the curb. Deliberately, she straightened her spine, pushed her shoulders back and her chin up. "We need to find a phone."

"We need to get away from here," Ethan said.

"That too." Mel looked up at Ethan. "I'm sorry your truck is gone. It could have been towed, not stolen by Derek's men. Or stolen by someone else who found your key."

Ethan shrugged. "Not sure it really matters either way. The end result is the same."

They began to walk…trudge, more like it. Mel wasn't sure if going back to the office was a good idea, but it was her best option. If Megan or Jessica wasn't in the office, she could call one of them for help. The office had plenty of phones. She could call the police, too, but wasn't sure how much good that would do at this point. They could report the truck stolen, yes, but the cops couldn't do much about that. Stolen vehicles were a dime a dozen in the city. Otherwise, the three of them were free but could prove nothing. They didn't know where to find the men who had chased them.

At the office, Mel had supplies in her desk, things she hadn't used in months, like her Glock, along with more pepper spray, food, petty cash. Most of all, she had support there or at her fingertips.

"We'll go to my office," she said.

"Won't they be watching it, expecting us to go there?" Ethan asked.

"How far away is it?" Sheila asked.

"Not far," Mel assured her. To Ethan she answered, "Yes, they probably will. Someone should be there though. I mean Megan or Jessica."

"And how do we get past anyone watching?" Ethan asked.

"*We* don't." Mel gave him a look intended to say *Don't argue with me.* "*I* will go. You two will find a place to hide out like—" She glanced around, her mind suddenly blank as to what businesses were around. A building on the other side of the L tracks caught her attention and she nodded. "Perfect. Go to the Target. It's not very big, but it gives you lots of places to keep out of sight."

"I'd rather go with you," Ethan said. "But…" He glanced toward Sheila.

"Take care of your sister. I can go faster alone."

Ethan nodded, and he and Sheila set off down the block. At the corner, they turned to take the alley the rest of the way.

Hands in her pockets, hair flopping into her face in limp strands, Mel headed for her office, where everything had started such a short time ago. She wished Ethan was at her side, but she knew that they'd made the right decision. Not having him there was a better idea. Even without Sheila needing him, he stood out too much. He was over six feet tall and broad across the shoulders. Mel, on the other hand, was barely five foot four and presented a narrow profile. She could— she had—tucked herself into some narrow spaces to get out of harm's way.

Though she kept her head down, she never stopped scanning the sidewalk and street for signs of Derek's men or some kind of clue they were waiting to pounce like patient cats on a mouse.

She was used to being the cat, the hunter, not the hunted. She didn't like the vulnerability.

When she turned down the street leading to her office, she noticed an SUV rounding the corner behind her. Coincidence? Maybe. Pursuer? Probably. Only twenty yards to the office door. Lights were on. Someone was there.

She had to fight the urge to run. She had a plan that might or might not work, but she knew it was her best shot.

As she and the SUV drew parallel to her office door, Mel ran into the street, right in front of the SUV. She didn't think they would run her down. She hoped she hadn't miscalculated.

She hadn't. The vehicle slammed on its brakes. The passenger door flew open. "Stop!" a man shouted like he had at the L station, as though he expected her to listen to him this time.

She didn't. She turned toward him. He grinned, triumph shining from him, though his eyes were hidden behind those mirrored glasses.

Mel grinned back then dove beneath the SUV. She slithered on her belly, figuring her clothes couldn't get any filthier than they already were. If the driver hit

Reverse, she was a goner. But they needed her alive for now, a lure to get Ethan and Sheila back.

The SUV seemed a mile wide, her military crawl as slow as a turtle. At the last minute, she changed direction and exited from beneath the vehicle at the back, farthest from either door with a person behind it. In a flash, she was on her feet and sprinting for the office. She yanked the door open. The electronic bell chimed.

Abandoning their SUV in the middle of the street, the two men, accompanied by honking horns and shouted protests, charged after Mel. She forced the door closed and threw the dead bolts.

The door was glass. With enough force, it was breakable, but it was bulletproof. Two shots pinged off the glass, scarring it. But by that time, Mel had dropped behind the reception desk and was scurrying in a duck walk to the hallway, to the office cubicles, to telephones and weapons and food.

Jessica met her halfway down the narrow corridor. "What's going on?"

"Did you call the cops?" Mel glanced back at the door, the pounding reminding her of Ethan banging on the back door to get her attention, to get her help, just a few days ago.

Jessica, dressed today like she was about to go shopping, looked plain until she applied the correct makeup. She was a master at disguises. With the swipe of a makeup-cleansing towelette and the ditch of a wig, she appeared like a wholly different person. And she knew how to act. She had come from one of the major theater companies in the city. Having grown tired of not making enough money to live on, she'd put her talents to other uses.

Right now, she was playing the role of implacable, suburban, rich young matron. Her calmness seeped into Mel, giving her the moments she needed to catch her breath and let her heart steady.

"It's too long a story to go into. I—we—need help right now."

"The cops should be here any minute now," Jessica said. "What more do you need?"

"A way to get me and two other people out of town." Mel took a deep breath to explain more, but Jessica cut her off.

"Does Megan know about this?"

"Some. Yes. It's complicated." Feeling the agitation returning, Mel took a deep breath. "Jess, I need a car. Don't—" she held her hand up in a stop position "—ask what happened to mine. I borrowed a car from Megan yesterday, but… I had to leave it behind. My client's truck was stolen. A drug dealer wants his sister and him and, by association, me. In short, we need to get out of town now."

"Is that who's trying to break our front door down?" The faintest twitch had taken over Jessica's right eyelid.

Not so calm after all.

"It is."

They would succeed if they kept it up. Then again, if they kept it up, someone on the street might try to stop them. Police would be there shortly, no doubt. Mel thought she heard sirens. She must have. The pounding had ceased.

"I should get away from here as fast as possible. They want me, not you. You'll be safer with me gone."

"But what about you?" Jessica glanced around the nearby cubicles. "What can we get you? You look awful, you know."

"Thanks. I know. I mean I can guess." She hadn't paid attention to her reflection in car mirrors. She didn't want to know how flat her hair must be, how wrinkled and filthy her clothes were. She knew she felt grimy and sticky, and she didn't even try to smell herself.

"You should stay and talk to the police," Jessica said.

"I know, but I have to help Ethan and Sheila."

If they were safe.

"I need my gun," she admitted.

Jessica stared at her. "You want your gun?"

The sirens were definitely louder. Good and bad. They would hold Mel for hours, answering questions again, while Ethan and Sheila were helpless somewhere.

"Please, Jess, is there an extra agency car nearby?" Mel asked.

Jessica shook her head. "All at Megan's house. More parking there. But mine's parked a block away."

Mel looked into Jessica's eyes, willing her to make the offer Mel wouldn't ask. She knew what happened to cars in her care lately.

"You can take mine," Jessica said, reaching into her handbag. "It's not cool like yours, but it runs."

"You don't need it today?" Mel gave her colleague an out.

"I can take the L. I'm working in the Loop."

Mel was hopeful Derek and his men wouldn't know to search for Jessica's car. She doubted he had that much information about the agency.

"Thank you." Mel took the ring of keys Jessica handed her, removed the car fob, and handed the rest back. Then Mel slipped past Jessica to enter Megan's office.

Mel knew the combination to the safe. They all did. Most of them kept their weapons there when working in the office for any length of time. Her Glock lay in its case; heavy, black, deadly. A shudder ran through her as she lifted it. She hadn't used it in months. She never wanted to use it again, but she would if necessary to protect…others.

Mel also raided the office's petty cash box. It held more cash than most businesses would need, since some of their assignments required cash only to keep their movements untraceable. If she still had her purse, Mel would have written Megan a check then and there to refund the box. Since she didn't, she grabbed a sticky note from Megan's desk and scrawled an IOU.

Outside the office, the sirens had stopped. Someone was pounding on the front door. Mel squelched the guilt pressing on her for having Jessica handle matters instead of sticking around to deal with it herself. Right now, Mel needed to be gone.

Yet she didn't know how to exit. The cops would stop her at the front. Dangerous men might stop her at the rear, and opening that door would leave the office vulnerable.

No, Jessica would be all right with the police in

the office. The men would never enter. They would be too busy attempting to stop Mel.

Then she would simply have to find a way to stop them first.

She slipped a box of ammunition out of the safe, closed the door, and spun the dial. She needed a bag to carry things. The office kitchen might hold a stray grocery bag.

Mel snatched her sweater from the back of her chair as she passed her cubicle. It was soft and smelled of fabric softener. She wanted to snuggle into it and take a nap.

She moved on to the kitchen and found a reusable bag hanging from a cabinet door. The fridge yielded bottles of juice and water, and a drawer provided her with a handful of protein bars. That was enough. From the voices in the lobby, the police wanted to look through the office.

Mel needed to scoot.

She scooted. The back door's lack of a peephole loomed before her again. That needed to change. She would take care of it when she got back.

If she got back.

She would. She had to believe she would.

Bag of weapon and snacks hooked over one arm, a can of snatched pepper spray in the other, Mel yanked open the back door, ready for a fight.

The alley was empty. Even though many businesses were opening, not a single person moved through the space behind the buildings. The arrival of the cops must have scared the men away. Mel just had to walk to the end of the block and over to the next side street to arrive at Jessica's car. Easy. Too easy.

Trying to be alert to every movement within a hundred feet of her, Mel jogged down the alley and onto the sidewalk. Still no one within a block. A few people walked toward the more major roads or the L from where they had parked their cars or from apartments nearby. Mel couldn't tell if any of them didn't belong. Many were men. Many dressed all in black. A few wore mirrored sunglasses.

Muscles so tense she felt as though a blow would shatter her, Mel crossed the street in the middle of the block and entered the next alleyway. Still no one. The door to one building was open, with a woman sweeping a rear hallway. She called a cheerful good morning to Mel and kept sweeping. Mel waved and left the alley.

The side street was quiet. Jessica's car was much like Mel's had been—small, gray, nondescript. Hers just lacked a powerful engine. Mel doubted it could go zero to sixty in less than a minute. Not a great getaway car.

But she'd take any vehicle at this point.

Mel clicked the fob. The car chirped. Mel slid behind the wheel, set her bag of goodies on the passenger seat, and headed in the direction that would get her to the Target.

At the cross street, another nondescript gray car filed in behind her. By the time she needed to make her left turn, she was pretty certain she was being followed.

Ethan stood at the store window studying every car that passed, seeking a glimpse of a petite blonde behind the wheel. Unfortunately, dozens of cars passed and more than one carried a blonde lady behind the wheel. He had no idea if Mel would even show up in a car. She might be on foot. They hadn't taken time to make real plans for meeting up again, and making contact without a phone was hard.

Sheila wasn't with him. She had taken refuge in a ladies' dressing room. Ethan would fetch her once he reunited with Mel.

If he reunited with Mel.

About the hundredth gray or beige car passed. He homed in on those in particular because of Mel's car. She would try to find something similar, if she could find something at all. So far, seven of the gray or beige cars had a blonde behind the wheel. All had long hair, though, or the wrong color of blond. He sought the woman with hair like trapped sunshine.

Hoping to ward off inquisitive or suspicious store employees, Ethan stood with his arms crossed over his chest and a grim expression on his face. He was playing the role of someone waiting for another person who was late. Occasionally, he tapped his toe in a sign of impatience. The guise must have been working. No one had bothered him in the past ten minutes, not since sirens shrieked past, heading in the direction of Mel's office. Ethan wanted to know what the trouble was. Police on the way meant she had encountered a problem.

Of course, the sirens could be wholly unrelated.

He tapped his toe some more, this time from genuine anxiety not impatience. He and Sheila couldn't remain in the store forever, and he was truly stuck without help and without his truck.

He had to go to her office. He had no choice. Sheila

would probably be all right in the dressing room for a while longer. But people were starting to give him odd looks again.

He started for the door.

"Sir?" someone called. They were addressing him probably, but he chose to ignore it.

"Sir," the voice came again, "may I help you?"

With a sigh, Ethan turned... And Mel slipped around the end of a register aisle, looking tired and pale and beautiful to him.

"How did you—" he began.

She shook her head. "Not now. Where's Sheila?"

"Dressing room. But how—"

"Then let's go." Mel slipped between long aisles of goods and through racks of clothes until she entered the dressing room. A moment later, she emerged with Sheila hugging her arm as though she hadn't expected to ever see Mel again.

Ethan knew how she felt.

Once they were together, Mel drew them into the center of a rack of T-shirts and spoke in a low, rapid voice. "I have a car, but I was followed here. I parked and wandered around a little, then came in through the back. But I have no guarantee I've lost them, so we have one last chance. Would you rather go to the police or make an attempt to get out of Dodge?"

"I need to get home. I have to get to my boys," Sheila said, and started to cry. "Even if the police agree to help us, we'll be there for hours. Hours Derek could use to get to our sons."

Ethan needed to borrow some of that money Sheila said she had and buy a box or two of tissues.

"We need to go," Ethan said.

"All right, then we have to hustle."

"Where is the car?" Ethan asked.

"I parked it at the loading dock."

Ethan raised one brow. "Won't they move it?"

"Like I said," Mel said with a smile, "we have to hustle."

Ethan caught hold of each woman's hand, and the three of them made a chain to wend their way through towers and pallets of unopened boxes until they reached the wide doors of the loading area. A delivery truck was trying to back in on one side and something that might be a tow truck was headed their way.

"Keys?" Ethan said, holding out his hand.

"I should drive. You don't know where to go if we're followed," Mel protested.

"I'll figure it out. You, on the other hand, look like you're about to collapse."

"I can keep going," Mel protested again even as she pulled the fob from her pocket and dropped it into his palm.

He clicked the button, and a gray compact car flashed its lights. Mel's car had been small. This looked even smaller. His head was going to go through the roof, but he resolved not to complain. He didn't care how cramped he was so long as he was moving out of the city and toward the rest of his family to keep them safe.

Safe, right now, meant getting in that car. Several men were yelling and gesturing around the vehicle. Ethan shouldered his way into their midst and opened the passenger door for Sheila to climb into the back and Mel the front.

"Sorry, y'all," Ethan said to the men, "had to park here. An emergency."

The presumed driver of the truck and at least two store employees began yelling at him. Ethan merely smiled and climbed into the car. He had to get out of there fast. Besides, in addition to the three men saying rude things about him and to him for parking in a restricted area, there were also two other men leaning against the side of the building, appearing bored and idle, their mirrored glasses giving away nothing of where their eyes tracked.

Ethan didn't need to figure it out; he already knew.

He took a few seconds to push the seat back, then honked the horn to warn the men to get out of the way before he stepped on the gas. Unfortunately, the car didn't shoot forward. Its engine whined up to a decent revolution number and their speed gradually increased over a minute, two. They shot down the alley and around a corner.

"Watch for pursuit," Ethan said.

"They got a different car," Mel said. "One kind of like this one. At least I think so—I spotted a gray car following me here."

"Who were those men?" Sheila asked.

"Lookouts." Ethan took another corner too fast. The car swayed. For a moment, he feared it would roll. But it was more solid than the engine suggested, and they shot forward with all four wheels on the ground.

"If you go that way," Mel said, pointing, "you can get on Lake Shore Drive, Highway 41."

He didn't go directly the way Mel indicated. He drove them in zigzags and loops. Still, no one seemed to pursue them. They reached the highway running alongside the lake and headed south. The air smelled of fresh water, and he lowered the window, refreshed by this touch of nature. Traffic was heavy. If someone followed them, they wouldn't be able to spot the tail. At one point, he took an exit to see if anyone else did too. No one did, and he returned to the highway.

A few miles farther south, he exited again. Still no one.

After pulling to the side of the road for a minute, he looked at Mel. "Where do you think they are?"

"Ahead of us," Mel said. "I realized they don't need to follow us. They already know where we're headed."

"And Derek's going to get to my boys first," Sheila said.

SIXTEEN

Mel knew Ethan was uncomfortable. He seemed to be a man who talked only when he had something to say, and he was not a man who fidgeted. At least, she had yet to see him fidget—until now. He shifted in what had to be an uncomfortably low seat for him, drummed his fingers on the steering wheel, and glanced at her from the corner of his eye several times.

After an hour or so on the road, feeling herself drifting into oblivion, she finally touched his arm to draw his attention. "What is it?"

"What?" He started then shot her a quick smile. "Sorry. I, um…" He cleared his throat. "Were you able to get any money?" As he posed the question, his face reddened.

Mel nearly laughed at his discomfort, yet she knew she would be just as embarrassed if the situation were reversed.

"I did," she answered.

"Enough for us to get a room in a motel? As much as I'd like to keep going," Ethan said, "I think we need to stop somewhere and sleep."

"But the boys," Sheila protested. "Derek."

"I know, Shee, but we won't do the boys any good if I fall asleep at the wheel."

"I can drive," Sheila said.

"So can I," Mel said. "But none of us has had more than snatches of sleep or anything decent to eat in far too long. And that reminds me." She pulled protein bars and water bottles from her bag. "Let's stop when we see a lodging sign. We need gas too."

Ethan glanced at the gas gauge. "Shoulda looked. Empty's closer than I'd like."

Mel kept a lookout for an exit with a motel, cheap—she hoped—gas and food. They had entered Indiana, which she didn't know at all.

"We can get a map too," Ethan said. "I'd like to take some out-of-the-way roads when possible."

Less visible to others traveling in the same direction, and it would be easier to spot anyone following them.

"We should look for a store that sells cheap clothes," Sheila said. "We all look terrible. And a hairbrush. I'd shave my head for a hairbrush."

Mel nodded and kept searching for the right signs. The thought of clean clothes and even the lumpiest of cheap motel beds made her almost unbearably sleepy. The grayness of the day didn't help. Chicago had been sunny, but the farther southeast they drove, the thicker the clouds grew, from fluffy silver to misty gray to steel. Black thunderheads rose in the north, from the direction of the lake. She kept blinking. Keeping her eyes open grew harder and harder with the monotony of the highway.

Rain started about a half hour later, around the

same time Ethan announced the gas gauge was closing on E pretty quick. Both events jerked Mel from a
drowse just in time to spot the billboard she sought—
gas, food, and lodging.

"There," she shouted.

Sheila gasped, and Ethan slammed on the brakes,
earning them a blast of horns from behind.

"I'm sorry." Mel rubbed her hot cheeks. "I didn't
mean to startle everyone. There's what we want is all."

"I thought you saw Derek," Sheila muttered.

"Let's go then." Ethan flicked on the turn signal
and they drove along the strip of blaring signs pro-
claiming vacancies, gas prices, fast food.

They found the cheapest of motels and took two
rooms. Mel went into the office alone and paid in
cash. She hoped this would diminish their traceability,
even if she knew her bedraggled appearance would
make her too memorable. Nothing she could do about
it. This was the right move. They would collapse if
they didn't sleep and eat.

"I'll get us some food and bring it back here,"
Ethan said.

Mel reached into her reusable bag.

Ethan shook his head. "I have the money Sheila
managed to come away with." He smiled at his sister
as though she were the cleverest of women.

She glowed under his approval then turned to Mel.
"There's, um, one of those super discount stores across
the road." She gestured to the narrow road that separated the various establishments at this service area.
"I could get us some things, if…if…" She ducked
her head.

"Of course." Mel didn't know exactly how long

they would take to get to Kentucky. Surely not more than a few hours. Still, she needed to conserve what cash they had. On the other hand, Sheila was right about how awful they looked and how much they needed basic necessities.

She pressed some bills into Sheila's hand and told her her sizes. "Nothing fancy."

Sheila giggled and darted across the road, not, in Mel's mind, being as careful as she should have been when crossing the road in the rain.

The rain was their friend though. No one could see them clearly. Mel doubted even Derek would have recognized Sheila through the downpour and the grayness.

Mel stumbled into one of the two rooms and resisted the urge to throw herself onto the double bed. The room was clean enough. She didn't think she'd have minded if it weren't, she was so grubby herself. Things were simple—a tiny table and two rickety chairs, the bed, a nightstand, and a dresser with a chipped Formica top where a TV that had to be twenty years old was anchored.

The TV drew her. She hadn't watched the news in days. For some reason, none of them had turned on the radio in the car. Maybe they didn't want to know what was going on.

The motel was cheap enough that it didn't provide cable. Mel managed to tune in two local stations. Good enough. Except the news wasn't on. She had the choice between a soap opera and a talk show.

She settled on the talk show just for the human voices, realizing how much she hated the silence of the hotel room now that she was alone for the first time in over a day. The lack of human interaction reminded her of what her house was like. Empty. Lonely.

She sank onto the edge of the bed and dropped her face into her hands.

So this was why she had dived into this case in spite of all the warnings from Megan and from her own good sense. She had been alone so much since her father died and things had fallen apart with her fiancé. She had chosen to take on work in the office that left her alone there much of the time. She talked to few people except for strangers on the phone, and Megan and Jessica when they were in the office.

She was sick of being alone. She was sick of no one really needing her. At the same time, though, she was wary of putting herself out there and risking getting hurt again. In Ethan and Sheila, she had found two people—four, if Mel counted the two children—who needed help. By focusing on them, she could push past her fear. That was why she had plunged into the case headfirst without heed for the rocks she might smash into at the bottom.

Someone knocked on the door then slipped the keycard into the lock. The door swung open, and Ethan swept in on a blast of chilly, rain-soaked air. With him wafted the delicious aroma of hot food. Ice rattled in cups and paper bags crackled. Ethan grinned through the lines of fatigue on his face.

And Mel knew another reason why she had taken the risks of this case—the client himself. He had interested her from the beginning. Now…well, her feelings toward him were far more than mere interest.

She was still wary though. Helping him was one

thing, but trying for an actual relationship? How would that even work? Did they have anything to hold them together when they weren't dependent on each other for their safety?

The case would be over within twenty-four hours regardless of what happened next. She would drive Jessica's car back to Chicago and never see Ethan again. She would be free to take on more cases, more comfortable doing so even when danger was involved. She doubted she would face anything like the last couple of days again in her career.

The prospect of being fully back on the job should make her ecstatic. Maybe she was too tired and starving.

"My mouth is watering," she said.

"It's just fast food, but I got the healthiest options I could." Ethan set the bags on the table. "Sheila not back?"

"Not yet. She wants to make us look more respectable."

"She would." Ethan sank onto the edge of one of the chairs. "She lived on the street for a while when she ran off to Chicago as a teen. Now she hates being messy in any way."

"That's so sad." Mel thought a minute. "How old is she, if she ran away as a teen?"

"She's twenty-three."

Mel's brows arched. "No wonder—" She stopped, not wanting to be rude.

"No wonder she got mixed up with Derek? Yeah, he found her when she was just starting to realize how hard it was to get by. He 'rescued' her and then used her gratitude to manipulate and control her."

"She was only eighteen when she had the twins?"

"Seventeen, actually. Derek married her, for some reason. I guess he thought a family would make him look more respectable."

Mel shuddered with disgust.

"And she was pretty naïve, having grown up in little McClure and gone nowhere else except maybe Lexington once or twice."

"How small is McClure?"

"I think we're up to four or five thousand now." Ethan glanced out the window. "Here she is."

He stood to open the door for Sheila, soaked to the skin but looking triumphant with her arms laden with plastic bags.

Within the hour, Mel felt like a different person. She had eaten, showered, and donned the T-shirt and sweatpants Sheila had purchased. Her hair was clean, her teeth were clean, and the sheets on the bed appeared clean enough. She mumbled something to Sheila, who was brushing her long hair, and was asleep within seconds.

When she woke, the room was dark, and Sheila was breathing deeply on the other side of the bed. Mel glanced at the clock glued to the nightstand. Nine thirty. She had slept for six hours. She could definitely use another six, but this was enough for the moment. They needed to be on the road. An eight-hour respite was all they had agreed to allow themselves. They couldn't waste more time on sleep and showers.

Mel slid from bed and turned on the TV. The news should be coming on soon. She needed to know what was happening in the world. Her phone usually kept her up with the latest breaking news, but she didn't have it any longer.

Mindlessly, she watched the end of some drama that made little sense in the real world. Then the news came on with a "just breaking" notification. Mel poised on the edge of the bed, staring at the screen, waiting for that breaking news as though it would affect her life. After what felt like an interminable number of commercials, the anchor returned with the announcement of a murder in broad daylight near the Belmont L station. Three people were wanted for questioning. A man and two women.

Ethan grabbed what few belongings he had and left the motel room. Light shone through the curtains of Mel and Sheila's room, so they were awake. Good. He raised his hand to knock, and the door opened before his knuckles made contact.

"I saw," Mel said.

At sight of her, eyes wide, face pale, Ethan felt an odd impulse to wrap his arms around her and assure her everything was just fine. Or at least that it would be. And maybe comfort wasn't the only reason he wanted to wrap his arms around her. He'd only been away from her for a few hours, yet this moment of encounter felt like a reunion.

He clasped her hands between both of his, finding her fingers freezing. "Is Sheila ready? We've got to go…now."

"Five minutes," Sheila called from inside the room.

"You saw the news?" Ethan asked Mel.

She nodded. "Do the cops really think we had

something to do with the man's death? And which of the guys is it? How did he die?"

"The news was short on details, but from the picture they showed, I think he was the one who always wore the mirrored sunglasses."

"But why would they kill one of their own? Why would the police suspect us? And why would our attackers have all of this go down at a public station where there were sure to be witnesses who would contradict any evidence they tried to plant against us?" Mel asked.

"I don't know." Ethan rubbed her cold fingers. "I wish I did. I wish…" He shook his head. "All I can think is someone in the police department who's been paid off by Derek wanted to cast suspicion on us. It's a decent tactic to slow us down and get more people on the lookout for us."

"But we're well away from the city and in another state. That shouldn't slow us down much, should it?"

"I'm thinking this means they don't know we've left the city."

"But they know the car. Someone followed me from Jessica's parking space—you saw them at Target."

"But they didn't follow us out of town," Ethan reminded her. "I hope this means they're behind us."

"Far behind us." Mel shivered and bent her head. "I don't want to encounter them on an open road like this. It's too…too remote. Too few people. Once we leave here, anything can happen."

"We'll be all right," Ethan said with more bravado than he felt. "We haven't noticed any sign of being followed out here."

He knew perfectly well that didn't mean no one was tracking them. On the other hand, the fact that no one had made a move on them while they'd rested gave him hope.

"Let's get food we can eat in the car," he suggested.

Mel nodded and returned to the room to retrieve her belongings. By the time she was done, Sheila was ready to leave as well. They closed the rooms, leaving the keycards inside. The rooms were paid for until the next morning. No one needed to know when they'd left, as Ethan had parked the car on the other side of the motel and out of sight from the road or the office.

A few minutes later, they were quietly munching on sandwiches and chips and drinking iced tea as they sped down the road. Beside him in the passenger seat, Mel took a long pull from her straw and started to cough.

He slowed the car. "Something wrong?"

"It has sugar in it."

"It's sweet tea," Ethan explained. "I'm sorry. I never thought you might not drink it."

"Everyone drinks it," Sheila declared.

"I might put lemon in mine, but we don't usually put more than a spoonful of sugar in our tea, if that." Mel set the cup in the holder on the console and reached into her bag, where she pulled out some water. "This will do."

Ethan smiled and, because they had a long ride ahead of them, he did what he had been wishing he could since he'd met her—asked her questions about herself.

"You've lived in Chicago all your life?"

"That's right—born and raised. My parents were cops, and they never lived anywhere else."

"Have you traveled anywhere?" Ethan asked.

Mel brushed chip crumbs from her sweater. "I've never been farther north than Wisconsin or farther south than Springfield, and I've never been east or west. My parents weren't much for big vacations. Why drive to a beach when we had them right there?"

"We never went anywhere either," Sheila said. "That's 'cause we didn't have any money until Ethan came back from the Middle East."

"I expect we didn't have much money either, though it wasn't something we ever really talked about," Mel said. "But we had a nice house and yard. I still live there." She caught her lower lip between her teeth. "I inherited it from my parents."

"Man, are they both dead?" Sheila asked.

"Sheila." Ethan warned his sister to be polite.

"Sorry," Sheila muttered. "It's just sad."

Mel nodded and turned her face to the window.

"So why a PI?" Ethan changed the subject.

Mel shrugged. "Being a cop has too many rules. I like more freedom."

"I get that." Ethan smiled. "Military life wasn't quite right for me in that way. Too many rules. But I needed something to make money, and the mountains aren't exactly full of opportunities. The coal mines are closing down. Farming is tough. We're too far away from cities for anyone to want to set up a company there."

"Horses?" Mel asked. "Isn't Kentucky known for its horses?"

"In the flatlands, yeah. Lots of horse farms. But

you can't really raise racehorses in the mountains. They're not the Rockies, but they're pretty rugged."

Conversation dropped. Sheila seemed to fall asleep in the back seat. Ethan had gotten a map at a gas station and studied the routes through the state. Southern Indiana was pretty rural, with long stretches of farms and forest. Once off the main highway, he felt like he could breathe again. Electric lights faded away. If the clouds cleared, they would be able to see the stars. Few cars traveled the same way as them at night, a hazard and a blessing. They would know at once if someone was following them.

"What about you?" Mel posed the question suddenly. "What do you do now that you're out of the army?"

"My parents owned a hardware store, but it was losing customers to the big-box stores. So when I got home, I took the service pay that I had saved and turned it into a general store." He laughed. "We get tourists, so I fill it with kitschy stuff tourists like. Lots of handcrafted things, too, though. That gets some money for local artisans. And I opened a café."

"That's right." Mel faced him again. "You said you make cupcakes."

"The best," Sheila murmured behind them.

"Simple stuff. Pies and soups and sandwiches. The café part barely breaks even now, but it's growing. But the store is…" He trailed off, fearing he was bragging.

"Successful," Sheila filled in. "Our dad carves things out of chunks of coal."

"You have both parents still?" Mel asked, eyes fixed on the rearview mirror.

Ethan flicked a glance to see what she was watch-

ing. Far in the distance, a faint glow suggested headlights.

"My dad isn't well. He worked in a coal mine for
twenty years, and that kind of work leaves its mark on
a man. But Momma's healthy and strong. She teaches
Sunday school and watches the boys."

"That's great." Mel sounded distracted.

Ethan understood why. The lights were drawing
nearer—fast. They were higher in the air than those
on their compact car. An SUV or pickup. Something
big. Heavy. Fast.

Despite the heater blasting in the car, Ethan shivered. No one needed to drive that fast on the two-lane
road. No one should drive that fast at night. Even if
it were some stranger who just happened to be in a
hurry, they would be able to see the taillights ahead
and know they were bearing down on the car.

It had to be intentional.

Ethan flicked off the lights. That would make them
more difficult to see. It also made seeing more difficult. Clouds darkened the night. No streetlights or
signs offered ambient light. He slowed and moved into
the opposite lane, the lane going the wrong way for
their direction. He just had to hope that there wouldn't
be any oncoming traffic.

"E-than?" Sheila's voice was plaintive from the
back seat.

"Hold on." He glanced at Mel. "Will you watch
them so I can watch the road and hopefully stay on
it?"

"Will do." She twisted sideways in her seat. "They're
about a quarter mile back."

Too close.

Ethan tried to picture the map in his head. He couldn't recall a side road anywhere. Maybe someone's driveway would show up. Maybe he'd forgotten a turn.

"About five hundred yards," Mel announced.

He loved the fact she could be that precise. He didn't love the nearness.

"It's a big pickup," Mel said. "Real big."

It could be a full-sized car and do them damage.

Ethan caught sight of a break in the trees and made a snap decision. He steered toward it. Foolhardy move, probably. He could drive them into a ditch. He could hang them up on a stump hidden in the darkness. He could strand them, make them sitting ducks.

"When we stop," Ethan said in as calm a voice as he could project, "take what you can and get out of the car and into the woods side as fast as you can."

"Whatever you're going to do," Mel said with the calm of someone discussing an upcoming journey, "make it quick. The truck is nearly upon us."

Fake calm like his own. Ethan nodded, then steered the car to the opposite side of the road.

"Ethan," Sheila screeched from the back seat.

Ethan ignored her cry and drove straight into the tangled brush and limbs along the highway. Branches snapped like gunshots. Limbs scratched the sides and roof. Then the front bumper hit something solid. The airbags blew. The engine ceased. Steam hissed from the radiator.

But the truck kept going.

"They didn't want us at all," Sheila said in a whisper.

"Don't…be…so sure." Mel gasped out the words, probably winded by the airbag.

They were already deflating, giving the passengers space to move.

"Grab what you can and get out," Ethan said.

"What are we going to do without a car?" Sheila asked.

"I don't know yet." Ethan figured he may as well be honest since the response was obvious.

He grabbed a bag of water bottles and road snacks, then stepped into underbrush.

Mel snatched the other bag of water bottles and shoved open the passenger's-side door. "Didn't we take this road specifically to avoid Derek's men?"

"We don't know if the truck was Derek's men," Sheila said. "I mean, they kept going."

"Only to turn around." With the three of them flanking the car, Ethan gestured toward the road, visible through broken branches and plowed vegetation.

The night was dark, so the lights seemed particularly bright.

The truck had turned around and it was coming after them.

SEVENTEEN

Mel resisted the urge to bang her head against the nearest tree trunk. If she stood on the other side of the wrecked car with Ethan, she would bang it against his shoulder. Or maybe simply rest it there. He looked so strong and solid, as though nothing would ever defeat him. He acted that way too. Strong, intelligent, kind— all the things she liked in those she worked with.

The sort one wanted for a partner. A work partner, she told herself. Nothing more once they settled things in Kentucky.

And that seemed a million miles away, nearly impossible to settle in triumph at this point, with their latest car undrivable, Derek's men coming back for them, and hundreds of miles left to their destination.

"They always figure out our moves." Mel scrubbed her fingers over her face. "I feel like I'm being tracked."

"Not tracked," Ethan said. "Just outmaneuvered."

"So we have to figure out how to countermaneuver." Mel drummed her fingers on the crumpled hood of the car. "We'll have to go deeper into the woods to have any hope of avoiding them."

"And we'd better do it quick," Ethan said with a glance toward the road.

The headlights shone brighter from a ways down the road. Maybe a quarter mile.

"I've only hiked in the forest preserves in Chicago," Mel said. "Those have paths. I don't think I could see a path here if it grabbed my ankles."

"There aren't any," Sheila said on a sigh.

"I'll do my best to make one." Ethan headed toward the tree that had stopped the car's forward momentum from the road.

Sheila fell into step behind him. Both were quiet save for the natural brush of feet and clothing through foliage. Mel pulled the handles of the reusable bag she'd retrieved from the foot well of the car onto her shoulder. It was heavy with the weight of several bottles of juice and water, not to mention her gun. When she joined the brother and sister in a hollow of space behind the tree, Ethan started to take the bag from Mel.

"I'll carry that."

Mel held on. "My Glock's inside."

Ethan ceased tugging. "You brought your gun?"

"I thought we might need it."

"But you hate guns." Ethan moved his hand from the bag handles to her cheek. "But you brought it to protect us?"

Mel shrugged, feeling an odd urge to turn her head and kiss his palm. "And me, of course."

"Thank you." Ethan stroked his thumb across her lower lip, then lowered his hand to the bag again. "You can have the Glock." He held the bag open while Mel pulled the gun and some extra ammunition from the bottom. She tucked the weapon into her waistband and the ammo in one pocket. It weighed her down, an unhappy burden.

She would be all right. She would be all right. She would…

She rested her hand on the gun, considering leaving it behind. Yet the night was black and still save for the approaching rumble of the truck's engine, and the surrounding forest looked as primitive and dangerous as anything found in a fairy tale. Reality as Mel understood it was bad enough. The woods in Illinois were full of coyotes and raccoons and the occasional bear. Bobcats weren't unheard of.

"Does a bobcat's cry really sound like a woman screaming?" Mel asked.

"Yes, ma'am, it does." Ethan's grin flashed in what little light the night provided.

Huh. Where was that light coming from?

Mel looked up to see an array of twinkling lights visible through the barely budding branches of the tree. They soared in a canopy above them. Twinkling lights hung by God.

Mel had seen a handful of stars before, but nothing like this, so pure and bright in the sky devoid of clouds now, washed clean by the earlier rain. Because she'd never seen more than a glimpse of stars, she'd never bothered to learn their names. They'd never needed names. They were simply glorious.

"Is something wrong?" Ethan asked.

Mel shook her head. "The opposite—something is right. I'm twenty-seven years old, and this is the first time I've been far enough away from light pollution to see just stars."

She scanned the sky but saw no moon. Just that glorious spread of stars.

"This is amazing." She smiled up at Ethan.

"Yes, it is." His voice was oddly rough. He smoothed his knuckles across her cheekbone, then dropped his hand to hers. "We can get going and the stars will come with us."

"Right." Mel lifted her hand to her cheek where he had touched it.

That had been the tenderest touch she'd experienced since her engagement ended. Except it felt far, far different. Her former fiancé's touch had made her feel secure, warm—up until she'd discovered he'd been lying to her. This touch made her feel…giddy.

Uh-oh. Another clue she should run from this man as fast as she could and as soon as possible. Except she worried that it was already too late. When she left him behind, when the case was over, she knew it was going to hurt to say goodbye.

She didn't let go of his hand though. She needed that anchor where she felt as though the three of them were the only people left on the earth. Logically, of course, they weren't. People had built the road. They would eventually get to a town and lights and a small population. For now, however, all she heard was the crunch of their soles on underbrush, the crackle of the plastic bag Sheila carried, and— A howl?

She shrank back as though the source of the howl stood before her. "What was that?"

"A coyote," Sheila said. "They're all over."

So casual about it.

"Will—will we run into any?" Mel asked.

"Probably not." Ethan tightened his hold on her hand. "They don't usually get too close to people."

"It's the wild dogs you have to worry about," Sheila said with a giggle.

"Shee, don't tease," Ethan said, but he didn't sound at all annoyed with her, maybe even a little amused.

"Wild dogs?" Mel asked.

"Yeah," Ethan said. "People dump their dogs in the forest when they've had enough of them for whatever reason, and they go wild. They learn to hunt and fight and scrounge and act like coyotes, only without the fear of humans coyotes generally have."

Mel glanced over her shoulder. "Maybe the highway would be a better goal?"

Sheila and Ethan chuckled.

"We're fine," Ethan assured her. "They look for lone people, if they look at all. It's the human dogs that concern me."

They began to creep through the trees and bushes. Each step from the three of them sounded like a thunderclap, or, with the crackling of dry underbrush, a building fire. After a few minutes, Mel felt as though she were walking in heat like a fire. Sweat poured down her face. She thought she was in good physical condition. Apparently hiking through untouched forest took a kind of athletic preparation she'd never heard of but suspected she'd feel for days—days when she would be back home alone.

She shook her head and stopped to wipe her forehead with the sleeve of her fleece jacket. The others stopped as well, still, not breathing, not moving.

"Do you hear what I hear?" Ethan asked.

"I don't hear anything," Sheila said.

Mel nodded, repressing a sigh. "That's because there's nothing to hear."

On the road a hundred feet away, the truck had stopped. Worse, the lights no longer shone, no longer let Mel and the others know where Derek or whatever men he sent after them were waiting. The men must also be listening, preparing to ambush Ethan, Sheila, and Mel.

Ethan knew the safest move now was to remain motionless and listen for the others. He wasn't sure if Derek's men knew these woods, but he suspected they weren't any more familiar with them than he was, possibly less. Ethan, at least, knew forests. Derek's men had appeared to be more comfortable in an urban setting. Eventually, sooner than later more than likely, they would make noise, show a light for navigation, do something to give themselves away. Ethan and his companions needed to be ready for that moment. Ready for what, he was still working out, rejecting the most obvious solution as too risky for Mel.

Then he felt her hand on his arm, her breath on his ear.

"I'm going to go reconnoiter the truck." Her lips brushed his ear.

Ethan shivered, though he was warm from exertion, and gave his head a vigorous shake. "No way. Too dangerous."

"I have a gun and know how to use it." She began to back away, to slip between two trees.

Ethan plunged after her.

And his knee gave out. He didn't step on anything untoward. He didn't bang the patella into anything. The muscles around the artificial joint, battered and over-worked the past couple of days, simply gave out and he went down in a pile of broken limbs—fortunately not his—and vegetation that crunched like a thousand broken eggshells.

In a flash, Mel spun toward him and dropped to her knees. "Are you all right?"

"I will be." She gripped his shoulders, her face mere inches from his, and he could almost forget about his knee. "Just overworked it a little."

"I'm so sorry. I wasn't thinking." Even in a whisper, her voice sounded throaty, as though she were about to cry. "We should have found you a walking stick. We should have hidden you somewhere while we—"

Rather than argue with her self-recriminations, Ethan kissed her. He'd been wanting to kiss her prac-tically since he'd met her, he realized in that moment with their faces so close. She was kind and thoughtful and smart and capable and…everything he wanted. He hadn't stopped to think about what he was doing at all and, within moments, was questioning whether he should pull away, whether this was something she wanted. He should have asked first—would have, if his brain had been working at all.

But before he could pull away, he realized that Mel was kissing him back, without hesitation, as though she, too, wished for the contact.

"I think," Ethan murmured, "we need to talk about this. Unfortunately, not till later."

"There's no talking about it." Mel drew back, sit-ting on her heels. "My home, my work, are in Chi-cago. Your life is in Kentucky."

"We'll talk later," Ethan began. "Right now—"

"Y'all," Sheila murmured, "I hear them coming."

So did Ethan. The footfalls were stealthy, a mere whisper of feet through brush. The footfalls of a man who knew how to move in woods with little sound. A hunter not wanting to forewarn his game. He was probably good at tracking deer or pheasant. At that moment, he hadn't needed much help to find the three of them, from all the noise Ethan's fall had caused.

Sheila was good at hunting, too, and had caught the hint of sound in time to warn them.

"We need to run," Sheila said.

"Too late." The man's voice filtered through the foliage like a loudspeaker, as he turned on a Maglite. "I've got you."

"Not quite," Mel said, and extinguished the light with a single shot.

EIGHTEEN

The man yelled and Sheila screamed at Mel's gunshot. That made finding him easy. As her eyes readjusted to the mere glimmer of light, Mel picked out his silhouette from the surrounding trees and pointed her gun center mass.

"Give Sheila your gun," Mel said.

"I won't—"

"This is a Glock." Mel interrupted his objection. "No safety and I'm a little nervous here in the woods at night. I hate those coyotes. If one howls again, I just might shoot by accident, so the sooner we're out of here, the better for all of us."

As though on cue, a yipping sound pierced the woods. Probably a fox, Mel thought. Or one of those wild dogs. No matter, a thud hit the ground near the man.

"Pick it up," Mel said, "then search him."

"I got it, Shee," Ethan said.

With some grumbles of protest from the man, Ethan searched him, announcing what he found. A knife. A wallet. A cell phone. "And a pile of zip ties." Ethan laughed. "Did you all invest in these?"

The man said something rude.

"There are ladies present," Ethan admonished him.

"Ladies don't know how to shoot guns."

"We do," Sheila said. "I can shoot the feathers off a duck at a hundred paces."

"You won't be shooting nothing when Derek gets ahold of you."

Sheila let out a little sound like a sob. From a few moments of bravado, she returned to the terrified young woman she had been earlier, gasping for air like she was having a panic attack.

"Let's get out of these woods," Mel said. "Sheila, lead the way to the—" Mel interrupted herself. "Who's with you?"

"And where is he?" Ethan added.

"Wouldn't you like to know," the man sneered.

"You sound like a third-grader," Mel said. "But I have a full chamber here says you better hope he doesn't try to harm any of us."

"In fact," Ethan said, "Let's contact him from your cell phone."

A cell phone. Gold to them.

"Doesn't work out here." The man sighed. "He's in the truck waiting for my signal."

"Which is?" Mel asked.

"Three sharp whistles."

"And what will he do then?" Ethan asked.

"Go open the back of the truck." The man sounded weary, as though he no longer cared what happened.

Maybe he didn't.

"Then whistle," Mel said.

They wanted the other man out of the vehicle, more vulnerable in the open.

"And if you've lied to us," Ethan said, "I now have your gun."

Mel doubted Ethan would execute the man any more than she would, but if he thought they were angry enough to do so, that was what mattered.

Angry or scared enough to do so. At that moment, Mel wasn't sure which she was. Maybe both. Angry with Derek for his greed and willingness to harm his former wife and use his children for his own gain, and frightened at how far Derek would go to get his own way.

Well, she would go pretty far to get hers. She had proven that already.

And so had Ethan. Kissing her to make her stop blaming herself for his injury. Kissing her to distract her. Kissing her because… Because…

When they reached the road, Mel told Sheila to wait inside the trees with her brother and their prisoner. Sheila did so while Mel slipped around the front of the van and approached behind the second of Derek's hirelings.

"Hands up," she said, pushing the muzzle of her gun into his spine.

He cursed and tried to run.

Mel sent a shot winging over his head. He hit the ground facedown, hands behind his head as though he had gone through such a situation in the past.

"Don't move," Mel commanded. "Sheila? Some of those zip ties, please."

Sheila secured the man's wrists and ankles. Ethan secured the other man.

Once they were both resting on a pile of brush at the side of the road, Ethan asked, "Who are you?"

No answer.

"How many of you are there?" Ethan tried again.

No answer.

Mel, Ethan, and Sheila headed back to the truck.

"You can't leave us here," one of the men shouted.

"We'll let the police know where you are," Ethan said.

Shaking, Mel climbed into the passenger's-side front seat. For a heartbeat, she held her gun as though it were a baseball, yearning to toss it into the trees. She had vowed to never use it again, but she had used it to threaten. She'd fired it twice to frighten, breaking her vow to herself.

And, in case she had to do so again, she secured the trigger and slipped the weapon into her waistband.

Ethan made sure Sheila was comfortable in the rear seat of the cab, then swung into the driver's seat. Pushing the gas pedal wouldn't make his knee feel particularly good, and he didn't care. They were on their way again, headlights bright, illuminating the narrow ribbon of road leading back to the highway.

"How many men does Derek have working for him?" Ethan asked Sheila.

"Four. It's always four."

"Then we only have two more to contend with." Ethan puffed a breath of released tension through his lips. "Plus Derek himself," he added.

"Three down," Mel said from beside him, her voice quiet and a little rough.

"Three?" Ethan asked.

"We're forgetting the man on the news," Sheila said. "They showed his face. He was one of them."

"So one to go plus Derek." Unless Derek hired someone else along the way, or had work parties in groups of four, or reached the boys first and had the best of deterrents from anyone coming near him. In that case, the country sheriff and his sparse corps of deputies, Ethan and five women like Mel wouldn't stop him. Not without skill Ethan wasn't sure any of them possessed or they wouldn't have been outmaneuvered so often.

But they had done the outmaneuvering this time, which made him feel just a little elated.

Until he caught a gasp and a sniffle from the seat beside him.

"Mel?" He held out his hand to take hers so he could keep his eyes on the dark road. "Is something wrong?"

Silly question.

Under other circumstances, Ethan would have laughed at himself. For that moment, he tried to amend his question. "I mean, obviously lots is wrong, but, well, you're not crying, are you?"

"Of course not. I never cry."

"I wish I didn't," Sheila muttered.

"You seem distressed," Ethan said.

Mel's laugh was shaky. "Gunfire. I fired my gun. I promised myself I would never do that again."

"I'm sorry you had to this time." He wished he could stop and hold her close. He wanted to kiss her again. But they needed to keep moving, and he probably shouldn't have kissed her in the first place. Still, he couldn't bring himself to regret it. Not when he knew how deeply he cared for her. He couldn't be sure that she felt the same way, but he knew that he wanted to find out.

He laced his fingers through hers and held on as long as he could. He held her hand until the curve of the road required both hands on the wheel. Then he held it again until they entered a town. Quiet though the town still seemed, he needed to apply both hands to the wheel again.

If they had crossed the Ohio into Kentucky, he would have located the nearest police station. He did not, however, want to get held up in Indiana explaining everything that had happened on the deserted road or in the woods. Time for that later. He still had a four-hour drive ahead of him to get home.

Sheila fell asleep in the back seat. Mel seemed to do the same in the front, slumped against the window. He would have liked the radio on for company but didn't want to risk waking either woman. They had been through far too much this week.

At last the Ohio River stretched before him. Once across, he experienced the same sense of peace he always did when headed home, when driving toward the mountains. The air seemed fresher, the grass greener. He knew it wasn't true, but this was where he belonged, among people he trusted.

Mel woke about fifteen minutes after they crossed I-75 north of Lexington. "Can I drive for a while?"

"Have you ever driven in mountains?" he asked.

She gave him a look so annoyed he laughed.

"Didn't think so." He touched her cheek. "But when we're awake enough, let's talk about what we might find once we get to McClure and what we can do about it."

"What do you think we'll find?" Mel asked.

"Trouble."

Ethan stared ahead at the road, then up to the hills and the mountains beyond, so old they were worn down by thousands of years of wind and rain. Rocks and trees covered the slopes, and the rising sun gleamed gold in the passes and between the peaks.

Home.

"How far?" Mel asked.

"Another hour."

"We haven't seen a town since Lexington." Mel's nose was glued to the passenger window. "I think there are people out there somewhere though."

"Lots of them. Rich people with nice houses and poor people without running water—plus some people in between. And lots of wildlife."

"Coyotes? Bobcats?"

"Yes, and hawks and eagles and cardinals."

"Bears?"

"And foxes and deer."

She turned her head to smile. "You win. It's…kind of amazing." Her tone held awe.

"This isn't the best of it. Just wait."

While they drove, Ethan described his home, the town, and the surrounding countryside. They tried to figure out what Derek would do. If Derek was ahead of them, if they could get help.

"Once we're in town, I can go to the county sheriff. He's a good man. He'll listen. My dad has probably already briefed him on the situation."

They had used the confiscated cell phone long enough to let the state police know where the men were located, then Ethan had called his parents to tell them what was going on. After that, they left the phone at a rest stop, fearing Derek might have a tracker on it.

"But we'll need to be updated," Mel said.

"But if Derek has the boys…" Sheila began, then trailed off.

None of them seemed able to talk about possibilities, after all. They couldn't plan anything without knowing what they faced.

"He wants to take them away from me." Sheila spoke up. "He wants his money, and he wants his children, and I won't let him have any of it." She sounded fierce. "We have to stop him."

"We *will* stop him," Ethan said. "If it's the last thing we do."

The road grew steeper, climbing, climbing, until they crested the mountain and the valley spread out before them all gray rocks and rich earth and budding trees. And in the middle, the town nestled toy-sized from that distance.

But nothing about the traffic flying up the far side of the mountain was toy-sized, especially not the two sheriff cars with lights flashing and sirens wailing, blocking the street and waiting for them.

NINETEEN

They had found the trouble they'd expected. Two police cars in an area of light population meant something huge was afoot.

Mel snatched her Glock from her waistband and laid it across her knee. She wasn't sure of how her license to carry transferred in Kentucky but wasn't going to take chances without the despised weapon when she might need it most. The sight of it made her feel queasy.

Beside her, Ethan pulled to the side of the road in front of the waiting cars. Four deputies and a man who appeared to be the sheriff himself stepped from the vehicles, all carrying sidearms. Two men carried rifles. Something about their look, tall and lean, with a confident lift to their chins, told Mel they knew exactly what to do with those rifles. All the officers appeared fit and as stony-faced as the mountain on which they stood.

One rifle pointed at the truck as Ethan pulled up behind the official vehicles.

"They aren't going to shoot us, are they?" Sheila sounded nervous.

"We'll be cooperative," Ethan said. "Mel, your Glock. Get it out of sight for now."

Mel slipped the gun back into her waistband beneath T-shirt and hoodie. Part of her was happy to have it not close at hand. The other part felt too vulnerable without it.

"I'll tell the sheriff you have it," Ethan said. "I wouldn't call him a buddy, but we're on friendly terms." Ethan turned to Sheila. "Just be polite and don't flirt with Deputy Longerbeam."

Sheila actually laughed. "He's more likely to flirt with me." But she was blushing.

Mel arched her brows. "Something going on there?"

"The older deputies know me as trouble," Sheila said. "The younger ones think of me as…" She ducked her head.

A pretty, unattached young woman in a place where choice couldn't be all that abundant.

"It's the ones who think you're trouble we need to worry about," Ethan said.

"But I am trouble." The moment of levity passed with Sheila's confession. "None of this would have happened without me throwing away everything Momma tried to teach me."

Someone knocked on the front window at the same time, making "Lower the windows" motions.

Ethan complied, taking care of both from the driver's-side panel.

"I'm going to need you to—Miss Sheila?"

"Yeah, Billy, it's me. And you know my brother, Ethan. And this is our friend, Melissa."

The man on the other side, a man who reminded

Mel of her father, frowned at her. "What is your business here, ma'am?"

"I'm a private investigator from Chicago who's been helping the McClures," Mel said.

"Saving our bacon more than once," Ethan said. "So, what's going on?"

"We thought you were gone." The sheriff appeared at the side of the truck. "We were afraid you were... gone."

"Now I hate to tell you..." The sheriff glanced at Sheila.

"I know." She gripped the back of the seat in front of her. "It's my boys."

The sheriff nodded and the other men looked away.

"Your parents told us about your phone call, that you were worried about an attack and we had a deputy watching their house—but someone must have snuck around the back. When your parents woke up this morning, the boys were gone," the sheriff explained. "There was a note..." He cleared his throat.

Mel feared Sheila would begin to wail. Instead, she spoke in a voice that was cold enough to lower the temperature of the truck by ten degrees. "What did that note say?"

The sheriff heaved a sigh, his barrel chest nearly doubling in size. "It said you must turn yourself over to them, or turn over the money, or they aren't responsible for what happens to your boys."

"Of course he's responsible," Ethan all but growled. "He took them."

"And who is this individual?" the sheriff asked.

"My ex-husband." Sheila pressed the heels of her palms to her eyes.

"And his one remaining henchman," Mel added.

She refrained from saying, *If he didn't manage to gather more*. Unlikely in so short a time.

"Where am I supposed to turn myself over to him?" Sheila asked.

"We can't let you do that, Miss Sheila," the deputy they'd called Billy Longerbeam declared.

Sheila lowered her hands to glare at him. "You can't let me save my babies? What kind of a monster are you?"

"I, uh, I just meant…" His face turned fuchsia, and he ducked his head so fast his hat fell off.

"We're going," Ethan said, releasing the door latch.

"I'd like to deny you access," the sheriff said, "but if you're there, it'll show we're trying to negotiate in good faith."

"Where are we supposed to turn Sheila over to him?" Ethan asked.

"The Bridge," someone said.

Color drained from Ethan's face. In that moment, he looked three decades older than his years. A vein pulsed in his temple, and Mel wished to smooth it into calm with her fingertips.

"What is 'the Bridge'?" she asked.

"It's a natural bridge," Ethan explained. "Over thousands of years, the river carved a gorge through the mountains, except in one place, the land overhead didn't wear away. It made a bridge of sorts."

"With water flowing hundreds of feet below," Sheila added. "He's risking killing my boys."

"What can I do to help?" Mel asked.

"Stay right here, ma'am," the sheriff said.

"You expect me to—" Mel snapped her teeth together.

She didn't know these people. For all she knew, they would toss her in jail for getting in the way. She knew better than to interfere with an official police action. Yet she couldn't leave Ethan and Sheila on their own.

"We're with these men," Ethan said to her. He really had to stop reading what she was thinking. "These are all good men," Ethan continued, taking both of her hands in his. "Trust them. I do."

He might, but trust didn't come so easily to Mel, especially when a drug dealer criminal like Derek was so far outside the scope of what these men usually dealt with. The deputies and sheriff might be the best men in the world, but that didn't make them the best cops in the world, especially in a delicate negotiation.

"The FBI is here negotiating," the sheriff said, as though he read Mel's mind. "Because it's a kidnapping. Because you were kidnapped first, Miz Sheila."

Ethan handed her the keys to the truck, then he and Sheila followed the officers to one of the patrol cars. It took off up a road so narrow Mel wondered what would happen if another vehicle met them from the opposite direction. How could anything drive that close to vertical?

She was going to find out.

She slid into the driver's seat, maneuvering over the console with some difficulty, and rested her elbow on the doorframe. "So where is this bridge?" she asked Billy, who still stood beside the truck.

"Thattaway." He gestured up the road. "Road

splits. One way takes to the land bridge and the other takes to a real bridge."

"Yeah, I wondered if you could get across this gorge."

"Sure can." He retrieved his hat from the road, shook off the dust, and clapped it atop his dark blond hair. "People gotta get over there."

"Why?"

He gave her a look like she was being silly. "T'get home."

"People live up there?"

"Yes, ma'am."

"But—but don't they get snowed in?"

"Nah, snow don't last long here. Never more'n a week or so."

"I'm cold now and it's April." Mel shuddered and turned on the truck to be able to use the heater.

She glanced toward the other squad car. The deputy leaned against the hood, sipping from a thermos and gazing into the distance. Not an immediate problem. Getting Billy away from her car, on the other hand, could prove problematic if he didn't cooperate.

She gestured toward the other deputy. "Is that coffee? If so, may I have a cup? I haven't had any since yesterday, and it's killing me." She turned on her best northern Midwest twang for extra effect.

But, of course, Billy was as much a gentleman as Ethan had been. He wouldn't deny a lady anything if he could provide it.

"We got more in the cruiser," he acknowledged. "I think we can spare you a cup."

"Thank you. Thank you. Thank you." She smiled. Every word was truth. Watching the other man drink his coffee, she was pining for some. She was also grateful Billy was moving away from the side of her vehicle for just a couple of minutes.

The instant he ducked inside the squad car, Mel yanked off the parking brake and stomped her foot on the gas. The truck shot forward, swerving around the cruiser in a graceful arc, and then to the right to begin the climb uphill. And up and up and up. Mel feared coming down. She would be sick for sure. The road was so steep, she barely saw it over the hood of the truck, shiny black in the morning sunlight. She felt like she was taking off in an airplane, though she had never flown. She had, however, seen them climb in a nearly vertical soar like this one.

After a few minutes, she checked the rearview mirror long enough to notice the squad car coming after her. Its engine wasn't as powerful as the truck's, and the smaller vehicle was struggling. Mel put on a little more speed. A little more… A little more…

The road split. She swerved right without slowing down. The truck fishtailed, spitting gravel like hailstones, and that was when Mel noticed that only one side of the narrow road had land beside it. The other side was a drop so sheer she couldn't see what lay below. And no one had put in a guardrail.

Despite being followed, she decreased her speed and hugged the far side of the road. Walking would be safer. Nothing would make that road safe in winter. One patch of ice and it would all be over.

Her stomach rebelled at the idea of crashing into the gorge, so she pulled over to the side of the road. She would walk from here. She couldn't possibly keep driving under these conditions.

And then the track ended where a stand of trees began. They were stunted and twisted, but still oddly beautiful. Beside them, a narrow wooden bridge crossed the gorge. A wooden bridge her truck never would have able to cross anyway.

Mel crossed it, pretending it wasn't swaying in the wind that howled through the tapered canyon. She didn't want to know how far down lay the bottom yet couldn't help but find out. Gaps as wide as her hand stretched between many of the boards. Those gaps showed the faintest glitter of water rushing below—water that hustled so fast, it appeared to be constant rapids. And maybe a whirlpool.

Lake Michigan got some mountainous waves at times, but it never looked as dangerous as that distant river.

At the far end, Mel resisted the urge to fall to her knees and give thanks she was on land again.

Conscious of how Derek's remaining henchman could await her at any dip, clump of shrubbery, or curve in the path, expecting someone to do exactly what she intended, she started in the direction of the land bridge. She could see it winding in a graceful arch from one side of the gorge to the other, a span worthy of a cathedral roof. For a moment, she stood motionless in awe of the grace and beauty of the natural structure God had created.

Then her eyes focused and she saw three people standing at the top of the arch—one tall and two small.

Derek had taken the boys onto the bridge.

Mel did fall to her knees at this point. She didn't want him to see her. She didn't want the sheriff and his companions to see her, but they had reached the lane on the other side of the canyon. An agent might have gone ahead of her, ready to shoot first, ask questions later. She didn't think so, but she hadn't thought this entire case would turn into such a debacle of danger and death.

Two potential adversaries ahead, though the one shouldn't be against her. He just wouldn't know they were on the same side. That and the sheer drop to a rushing river were enough to give her vertigo, to make her sick.

She proceeded with caution. Through vegetation a yard or more high, she began to crawl. Thistles stuck in her pants and hands. Thorns ripped at her hair. Yet the smell was incredible, fresh and sweet and far better than any department store perfume counter.

She was moving close to the natural bridge. Snatches of words reached her on the buffeting wind. Mostly she caught the word *no*. No, Derek wouldn't get Sheila. No, he wouldn't let the boys go. No, he wouldn't believe the money was gone. No, he wouldn't believe Sheila had lied about having the money in the first place.

Mel suspected those were the words being shouted across the gap between Derek and his sons and their mother, along with her brother and law enforcement. Derek was intractable, and his sons, in such a precarious position, were effective pawns.

When she reached the end of the natural bridge, Mel knew her half-formed idea was unfeasible. The rock formation was only five or six feet wide and far from smooth. Besides sloping up to the center, the stone had been worn from wind and weather to create ruts and jagged outcroppings. If one were careful, those made great hand- and footholds. Caught in the wrong way, they could startle one into sliding over the edge. A sign at either side proclaimed it was property of the State of Kentucky and crossing it was trespassing. Those caught would be punished to the extent the law allowed.

If they survived and didn't get their punishment elsewise.

Mel figured she'd rather confront an angry deputy than an angry drug dealer, but at that moment, the latter was what she had to face. Rather, she had to hope he kept facing his former wife and others.

She began to crawl across the bridge. Up the bridge. She kept her eyes aimed on the man and two little boys. The twins' hair color was the same as their mother's caramel locks, and they had builds that already promised they would grow to have their uncle's stature. They were crying quietly, not wailing, just allowing tears to slide down their round cheeks. Occasionally, the word *momma* emerged from one of them, the sound carrying through the thin, still air.

She was so focused on what she could see on the bridge, she nearly missed the man crouched in a thicket of wind-gnarled trees a dozen feet from the edge of the gorge. He appeared no more than a shadow in his dark clothes. But the minutest of movements, the shift of a foot or hand, sent enough of a flash of light glinting off a gun barrel or lens of some sort to give the watcher away.

Mel lay still in the vegetation, not daring to breathe for fear she had already given herself away. Yet maybe she should draw the man's attention to her and away from protecting his employer's back.

She took a deep breath and pulled her Glock from her waistband. The snick of the trigger guard releasing did the trick. The watcher swung her way, fired without a moment's hesitation.

The bullet buzzed past Mel's left ear. Instinct told her to drop. Necessity kept her kneeling. Gun in both hands, steadied.

She fired.

The man screamed and slumped to the side. Mel left cover long enough to race forward and collect his gun. She sent it sailing into the gorge, one less weapon to harm anyone.

"You'll live to go to jail," she told the gunman.

She was a good shot. She'd hit his forearm exactly where she had wanted to. He might lose the use of his right hand, but he wouldn't lose his life or the opportunity to pay for his crime of working with and for a drug dealer.

Now she had everyone's attention, from Ethan and Sheila and the agents on the other side of the bridge, to Derek and the children on the bridge.

"Go back," one of the men she presumed was an agent shouted.

Mel ignored him. "Hey, Derek," she called as she stepped onto the ancient rock of the natural bridge, "you need to hire more competent men. I just took out your last one."

Derek faced her, gun drawn.

"What are you doing here?" he demanded.

"Stopping you, of course," Mel offered with a grin. She sat back on her heels, one hand behind her as though for balance, but instead concealing her Glock. "I'm that PI who's been giving your men so much trouble. This is literally my job."

"You." He spat on her.

"That wasn't very nice. But I suppose neither is this."

Mel lifted the muzzle of her Glock and sent a shot flying over his head. He jumped and dropped his weapon.

"Crawl back to land," Mel called to the boys.

From the corner of one eye, she saw Ethan moving onto the bridge to catch hold of his nephews.

Spewing vulgar language, Derek kicked at Mel's Glock. She backed up a foot out of his range and fired another warning shot over his head.

"At this point," she said calmly, "shooting you would be self-defense."

"Shoving you off this bridge would be self-defense," Derek claimed.

He fell to his knees and began scrabbling for his weapon. Mel's hand shot out and shoved it into oblivion. Derek lunged toward her, fists flying. One caught Mel on the side of the head. She ducked and rolled, tried to remain parallel to land. Her elbow came down on a sharp rock outcropping, and she jerked her arm up. Her finger pulled the trigger in reflex. Someone screamed. Mel didn't want to look. She had to look.

She opened her eyes in time to see Derek flinch from the blow of the bullet across his left side. The movement caused him to catch his foot in the hollow between two rocks and flip over the edge of the bridge.

Only then did Mel realize one of her legs dangled over nothing but space.

Ethan felt his heart leap into his throat as he saw Mel's leg dangle over the drop. Only a moment before, he'd been filled with relief to have his nephews safe, back in their mother's arms, but now…

If she fell, if he lost her, it would be like losing the whole world. He couldn't let that happen.

Running on the bridge was a terrible idea—everyone knew that. It was too narrow, too rough, far too dangerous. At the moment, though, he couldn't have cared less. He bolted over the length of the bridge as fast as he could, ignoring the screaming from his overstressed knee as he raced to get to Mel before she could go tumbling down.

The run seemed to take forever and just a second at the same time. He gathered her in his arms and yanked her away from the edge.

He was faintly aware that one of them was shaking, but he wasn't sure whether it was him or her. Maybe it was both of them.

"You're okay?" he kept asking over and over again. "Mel, are you okay?"

"I… I'm okay," she said, but her shaky voice made him question whether she meant it. "I'm okay, but he's…dead. He's dead because of me."

"Oh, Mel…my darling, no." Ethan tried to reassure her. "What happened to him is because of *him*. He made the choices that brought him here. None of that is on you at all."

But it was as if she didn't hear him at all. She pulled herself out of his arms and just kept looking down at the drop, as if she could see Derek at the other end.

Ethan's heart sank. He knew the burden she felt— knew from his military days about the weight it could leave on someone, that feeling of responsibility for the loss of a human life. He wished he had the words to comfort her, but he didn't know what to say. And moments later, the sheriff and his deputies approached and they were led away, separately.

He wondered if he'd ever see her again. He wondered if she'd ever forgive him for putting her in this situation, for leading her into this trauma.

He wondered if he'd ever forgive himself.

Mel sat alone at her desk, but she wasn't working. Not really. She was staring at the ridiculously large check that had come in the mail that morning and that Megan had told her to take care of.

Ethan McClure had far overpaid them for the work they had done. He'd said it was for the two cars they'd lost. But Jessica had insurance and Mel had insurance, plus she had found her car in a towing lot and been able to salvage the engine, the most valuable part. One day, she would find some way to put it into another car, and keep that piece of her father with her. Meanwhile, she was driving a motorcycle around the city because the weather was warm, and the smaller transportation form was easier to park.

Aside from that, her life had gone back to normal. Normal work, normal routine. And, just like normal, her house was still empty at night. But unlike before, what she felt when she was by herself wasn't just general loneliness. She didn't miss having *someone* around—she missed having *Ethan* around.

She had been back from her short trip to Kentucky for six weeks. After the deputy had separated her and Ethan and driven her back to town, she had been taken into the station for questioning. And once the sheriff was done, an FBI agent had showed up for more questioning. She wasn't allowed to see Ethan or Sheila but had been reassured the boys were well. The Chicago cops had lots of questions, especially in regard to the body found near the Belmont L station. So Mel had been summarily returned to Chicago like a criminal. In a short time, she had been cleared of any criminal charges and released.

After sleeping for a whole day and replacing her cell phone, she'd tried to call Ethan to ensure all was well with him. He hadn't responded, leaving her to wonder if she had been mistaken in thinking he'd had feelings for her. Her rational side told her to take the hint—to be grateful that Ethan had closed the door on anything more between them before she'd gotten too attached. It was for the best, that rational side of her said. There was less pain this way.

Of course, the rest of her wasn't interested in being rational and just knew that she missed Ethan. Yes, she risked some pain if she let herself love him. But surely that would be better than the pain and sadness that she felt on her own?

Her heart wasn't in anything. She worked like a robot. She slept because she had tired herself out.

She looked up the difficulty of getting a PI license in Kentucky.

Going out there would be taking a big risk and she couldn't be sure that it would pay off in the end. If Ethan wanted her there, he would have answered her with at least a text and not a check four times the size of his bill. But she had to at least try. And, hey, if she needed an excuse to talk to him once she was there, she could always take the opportunity to give him back the amount he'd overpaid. She would deposit the part of the check that she had actually earned and refund the rest.

She shoved it into a desk drawer and opened her laptop. With her PI experience in Illinois, getting licensed in Kentucky would be easy.

She laughed at herself for even looking but flipped to the website of the McClure General Store, now serving breakfast and lunch and the best cupcakes east of the Mississippi. Quite a claim. But they certainly looked delicious.

Mostly she looked at videos of Ethan giving a tour of all the handmade crafts they sold. Mel considered taking the extra payment from him and buying a handmade quilt for Megan and Jack's wedding gift. It was stunning, especially with Ethan standing beside it.

Tears blurred her eyes and she slammed the lid of the computer at the same time she heard banging on the front door. The front door didn't carry quite the same sinister associations as the back door, but banging like that was generally never a good sign. Every hair on her neck stood on end. Tingles raced down her arms, and she pulled her Glock from her top desk drawer, its resting place when she was in the office after hours.

The pounding continued.

Mel rose, gun in hand, and headed into the lobby. The glass in the door had been repaired. If it became necessary, she could run and call for help before anyone managed to break it down.

The lobby lights were off and the person at the door was backlit by streetlights. Tall. Broad. Chestnut hair.

She shoved the gun into her waistband and flicked open the dead bolts. The instant the door opened, she said, "We're closed."

"My favorite time for making a call." Ethan McClure stepped over the threshold. His hand reached out like he wanted to touch her, but he stopped himself before he could make contact. "You... I... It's really good to see you," he finally said. "Could I...maybe have a hug?"

She thought about it for a second and then stepped into his arms. For a few long moments, they just held on to each other. But then she pulled back, still in the circle of his arms and looked up at him thoughtfully. He certainly didn't look like a man who had no interest in her. In fact, he looked like a man who was using every ounce of willpower to keep from kissing her.

They needed to talk. They needed to figure out what they both wanted, and he needed to explain why he'd disappeared for six weeks, and they both needed to make it clear what they saw as the path forward for their relationship.

But just now, that could wait.

She lifted her hands to clasp behind his neck and then pulled his face down to meet hers. His kiss was tentative, then tender and wholly sweet. It was as sweet as that vegetation on the mountain had smelled.

"I hope that's my answer." Ethan raised his head and smiled down at her.

"Depends on the question." She tried to bat her lashes and flirt, but ended up grinning.

"You've missed me?" Ethan asked.

Mel held him closer. "You never contacted me."

"I was giving you space. You seemed really rattled at what happened to Derek. I was afraid you blamed me."

She stopped and thought about that. "I was upset," she admitted. "It was a hard situation, and I've spent a lot of time since praying about it, trying to come to terms with what happened. It's something I'm going to carry with me forever—and, honestly, I'm glad about that. I wouldn't want the loss of life to ever be something that's easy for me to handle. But while I regret that he died, I also accept that he was the one who put himself in that situation. And I'm certainly not sorry that he's no longer around to be a problem for Sheila or her boys. Or you."

"Then you really don't blame me?" he said, sounding totally vulnerable.

"No, sweetheart, I don't," she reassured him, going up on tiptoe to plant a soft kiss on his cheek. "I never did."

He gathered her up in a bear hug, squeezing her tight. "Thank you, thank you, thank you," he whispered in her ear.

"Wow, you really were beating yourself up over this, weren't you?" she said. "I was a little angry with you for the six weeks of silence, but now I get it. I have to ask, though, if you were so convinced that I blamed you, then what made you come here today?"

He released her and ran a hand through his hair, looking sheepish. "Um… Sheila may have kicked me out of the house and told me that she'd shoot my backside full of buckshot if I didn't come here and straighten things out with you."

Mel burst into laughter. "Well, that's a good bit more aggressive than I would have expected from your sister, but I have to say, I'm proud of her for showing such grit."

"I am too," Ethan replied with a smile. "So what do you say?"

"To what? You still haven't asked me a question," Mel teased.

"Okay, how about this then? Melissa Carter, from

the moment you opened your door to me, you've been exactly what I never knew I was always missing. I don't want to spend another day without you in my life. Please say that we can be together. I'll do whatever it takes to earn a chance with you."

"You already have," she murmured. "You've earned every chance you want. *You're* what I want. It's why I've been looking at licenses for PIs in Kentucky."

"We need a new deputy. The desk sergeant is retiring. The sheriff specifically asked me to ask you if you're interested in the job."

"Me work at a desk?"

Ethan chuckled. "That's what I told him. He said they could use your talents."

"And what about you?" Mel looked up at him.

"I'd rather not be shot or shoved into a basement hole."

"Or off a bridge?"

"Sure not my idea of fun."

"What is?"

He kissed her again. "Being with you. If you're not sure about Kentucky, then I can come here. I—I have been looking into hiring a manager for the store and finding work here. You said this is an all-women detective agency, but maybe you could use a man around sometimes?"

"I don't know about the agency," Mel said. "But I know I could. I mean, I could use one certain man around all the time."

His hold tightened until she could scarcely breathe. "I'm sure I can find something. In the city—"

She pressed her fingers to his lips. "I thought I loved being around all these people, but I realized I was just using the crowds and the bustle to feel less lonely. But it stopped working after I realized I'm in love with you."

"Are you saying you'll come to Kentucky with all the wild creatures and everything?" Ethan's face nearly glowed.

"I'll come to Kentucky with a man who loves me." She tilted her head. "If he does."

"More than anything, Melissa Carter. I love you more than anything."

* * * * *

If you enjoyed Abduction Rescue,
look for these other Love Inspired Suspense
titles by Laurie Alice Eakes.

Perilous Christmas Reunion
Lethal Ransom
Exposing a Killer

Find more great reads at www.LoveInspired.com

Dear Reader,

The past months have been a challenge for all of us. One solace I found lies in books. I read—everything. Love Inspired Suspense books, young adult books, self-help books, you name it and I probably read it. Books took me all over the country and sometimes the world, when I ventured only a few blocks for a walk outside my home. They also provided companionship when I felt all alone and isolated.

Thinking a great deal about isolation and loneliness, I have written this book about two people fairly happy with their lives, yet knowing they want something more. Melissa (Mel) yearns for a family. Ethan longs for peace and security for his family and himself. Individually, they have failed to find what they want. Together, they accomplish far more than either believed possible.

Laurie Alice Eakes

RESCUE MISSION
Rocky Mountain K-9 Unit • by Lynette Eason
Kate Montgomery thought coming to Montana would help her recover the lost memories she needs to find her friend's missing baby, but someone doesn't want her memories to return. K-9 handler Lucas Hudson and his dog, Angel, must protect her from a killer who will stop at nothing to keep their secrets safe.

IN A SNIPER'S CROSSHAIRS
by Debby Giusti
Attacked in an attempted car theft, taxi driver Lily Hudson plunges down a gorge to flee her assailant—not knowing that she's become his new target. Amish widower Matthias Overholt comes to her rescue, but when clues suggest the attacker is tied to a local murder, saving Lily again might be more than he can handle...

BLOWN COVER
by Jodie Bailey
While undercover investigating a suspected arms dealer, army special agent Makenzie Fuller blows her cover to save the life of her former partner, Ian Andrews. But he can't remember her or that he betrayed his country. Can he recover his memories in time to escape the killer's clutches alive?

EXPLOSIVE CHRISTMAS SHOWDOWN
Crisis Rescue Team • by Darlene L. Turner
Criminal investigative analyst Olive Wells must move quickly to catch a killer with an explosive agenda—because he's now targeted her. Suspecting the hit on his ex-fiancée is personal, will police constable Zac Turner and K-9 Ziva uncover the bomber's identity before he claims more victims?

WITNESS PROTECTION BREACH
by Karen Kirst
When his neighbor and her five-year-old son are attacked, mounted police officer Cruz Castillo is determined to keep them safe. But Jade Harris's escaped convict ex-boyfriend is set on getting his revenge—by abducting his own son. Will Cruz be able to see past Jade's secrets and protect her and her little boy?

ABDUCTION COLD CASE
by Connie Queen
Finding a mysterious file on her desk sends psychologist Kennedy Wells chasing down clues to solve a twenty-six-year-old kidnapping cold case—and straight into a violent assault. Texas Ranger Silas Boone safeguards Kennedy and agrees to help with the investigation, but the truth could prove deadly for them both...

_____

Get 4 FREE REWARDS!

We'll send you 2 FREE Books plus 2 FREE Mystery Gifts.

FREE
Value Over
$20

Both the **Love Inspired**® and **Love Inspired**® **Suspense** series feature compelling novels filled with inspirational romance, faith, forgiveness, and hope.

YES! Please send me 2 FREE novels from the Love Inspired or Love Inspired Suspense series and my 2 FREE gifts (gifts are worth about $10 retail). After receiving them, if I don't wish to receive any more books, I can return the shipping statement marked "cancel." If I don't cancel, I will receive 6 brand-new Love Inspired Larger-Print books or Love Inspired Suspense Larger-Print books every month and be billed just $6.24 each in the U.S. or $6.49 each in Canada. That is a savings of at least 17% off the cover price. It's quite a bargain! Shipping and handling is just 50¢ per book in the U.S. and $1.25 per book in Canada.* I understand that accepting the 2 free books and gifts places me under no obligation to buy anything. I can always return a shipment and cancel at any time by calling the number below. The free books and gifts are mine to keep no matter what I decide.

Choose one: ☐ **Love Inspired** ☐ **Love Inspired Suspense**
  Larger-Print   **Larger-Print**
  (122/322 IDN GRDF)   (107/307 IDN GRDF)

Name (please print)

Address   Apt. #

City   State/Province   Zip/Postal Code

Email: Please check this box ☐ if you would like to receive newsletters and promotional emails from Harlequin Enterprises ULC and its affiliates. You can unsubscribe anytime.

Mail to the Harlequin Reader Service:
IN U.S.A.: P.O. Box 1341, Buffalo, NY 14240-8531
IN CANADA: P.O. Box 603, Fort Erie, Ontario L2A 5X3

Want to try 2 free books from another series? Call 1-800-873-8635 or visit www.ReaderService.com.

LIRLIS22R2

HARLEQUIN
PLUS

Announcing a **BRAND-NEW** multimedia subscription service for romance fans like you!

Read, Watch and Play.

Experience the easiest way to get the romance content you crave.

Start your **FREE 7 DAY TRIAL** at www.harlequinplus.com/freetrial.

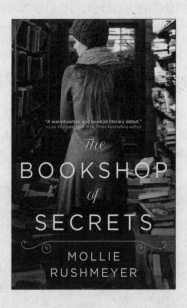